A Flight in Time

Andrea Hewitson

ISBN 978-1-916703-06-3

Typeset by Eleanor Baggaley
First Published 2024 by Snowdrop Publishing
www.Snowdrop-Publishing.com

For Mam, as promised.

Chapter 1

A Northern Blitz

Streaks of silver and gold lit up the sky and blood-red clouds of smoke billowed from the burning building.

People ran up the terraced street, shouting, panicking; the roar from the sky and the wail of sirens muffled their calls. Suddenly, part of the burning house simply crumbled to the ground. The rushing people turned, and hands flew to mouths; they stared, helplessly. Sirens wailed, and the rubble burned and glowed. Slowly, the roaring in the sky lessened and the sirens lost their voice. The German bomber retreated, its mission complete.

People stared and seemed frozen to the spot as the bricks crumbled down, and the smoke settled into dust. Within minutes, half of the end terrace had been demolished. The remains of the building stood —crooked and defiant, towering against the sky alongside a pile of smouldering rubble. Half of the house stayed intact, stubbornly standing: a wounded victim of a devastating war.

Chapter 2

War Wounds

Streaks of gold lit up the sky as the autumnal sun shone down, lighting up the end-terraced house. People busied themselves up and down the street; cars were lined up and parked on the road outside, and a family stared up at their new home.

'Well, that's it then. It's ours.' Jen stated, slightly surprised, mostly pleased. She placed her hand in her husband's, and they continued to stare at the house. Jen reached out to touch the 'sold' sign standing in its small front garden. Her husband continued to stare, and suddenly pointed upwards, towards the roof.

'I've just noticed it, just there ... look ... like the deeds said, "Repair due to wartime damage" ... there, look, the roof tiles and that sort of joining bit, in the brickwork. You can see the line.' Rob moved his finger as he pointed upwards to the join.

Jen shook her head and sighed, 'Look, Rob. It's structurally sound. And the survey said so, and it's ours. And, if it has survived a World War 2 bomb, then fingers crossed it can cope with us lot, eh? What do you think Archie?'

Archie shrugged his thirteen-year-old shoulders, looked up from under his hoodie, and screwed his eyes up, looking at where his dad was pointing. His dark hair spilled out from under the hood and he swept it away as if it was annoying him, quickly, returning his gaze to the ground. He muttered, ''S all right I s'ppose.'

His mam and dad exchanged glances. Rob joked, 'Steady on there, lad, you almost showed some enthusiasm!' He grabbed Archie's shoulder and gave him a shove, and Archie gave a slight smile in answer. He looked up at his dad, 'So? Are we going to McDonald's then?'

Rob and Jen looked at each other and exchanged thin smiles. The family walked back up the street, Rob and Jen taking turns to turn and stare back at their new home. Archie walked ahead, eyes cast downwards; he pulled his hood further over his head.

Chapter 3

Ghost Squadron

Boxes lined the walls of Archie's new bedroom. He had unpacked a few and their contents lay in random piles around his room: books, clothes and computer games were scattered on his bed and around the floor. He was busy searching through yet another box and suddenly, Archie smiled. He carefully picked a model aeroplane out of the box and placed it gently on an empty shelf which ran down the side of his bed. He returned his attention to the box and emptied it of another four models, each a World War Two aeroplane: Spitfires, Hawker Hurricanes, Lancaster bombers, carefully constructed and painted by him and his dad, usually on winter evenings at the kitchen table of their flat. His dad would go on and on about the planes, their history, their role in the war... and truthfully, Archie was interested, really interested.

Making the planes, feeling them in his hands, creating them, made history come alive for him—much more than dusty, stale history lessons with dates, facts, figures and battle names. His planes, his models - he could picture them in the sky; he could picture the pilots, hear the noise of the engine. He remembered his dad telling him stories about the famous battles and how dangerous the missions were. People, and real things, that was real history, to him, anyway. And if he did show an interest in history at school, what would his friends think? He'd be a laughing stock. So, this was his history. Archie picked each aeroplane up and turned it in his hands, admiring the details, the patterns, the shapes and the colours.

'Archie, your tea's out!' His mam's voice shattered his peace.

'Be down in a minute!' He called back, putting the Spitfire back onto his shelf, still staring at his collection.

'No, you'll be down now, before it gets cold! I know what your 'minutes' are like.'

Archie sighed and got up from his bed, thudding his way down the stairs. He walked down the thin hallway, lined with boxes, and into the dining room, where his dad was standing on a chair.

'C'mon, you can give me a hand before your mam starts the five-minute warning call again...' Rob was poking at the ceiling with a broom shank. He was tall, six foot or just over, and his jeans, checked shirt, and mop of dark hair were covered in dust. But the ceiling was high and Rob had to stretch to tap above him with the brush handle.

Archie looked around the dining room—it was empty of furniture and lined down the side with different-sized boxes. The floor was bare, and there were patches of plaster missing from the ceiling.

Rob talked as he was thumping the broom shank into the plaster, 'This ceiling's done in. We're going to have to get it redone, I think, but I just want to find out... stand there with the sheet and just catch any little bits that fall.'

Rob hammered the broom shank a little harder into the ceiling and suddenly, a crack formed. Plaster began to crumble and fall, covering Rob and Archie in white crumbs and piles of dust, and then, chunks of plaster tumbled down around them. Rob leapt off the chair and Archie stood, frozen to the spot, as the ceiling above where his dad had been hammering fell to the ground in pieces, with a crash. Rob grabbed Archie and pulled him aside. They avoided being pounded by falling plaster, but the avalanche continued.

Like a ghost, Jen seemed to appear in the doorway. Her blonde hair scraped back in a ponytail, was whitened with a layer of plaster dust. Her jeans and tee shirt had gained a layer of white dust too. She stared, mouth open, and Rob and Archie stared back at her: both of them zombie-like with chalky skin and whitened hair.

Jen started to speak, 'What the...?'

But Rob decided to seize the moment; he used the best-form-of-defence-is-attack strategy. He pointed a white dusty finger at her accusingly, 'I told you it needed doing, didn't I?'

Jen stammered out, 'Needed doing? A bit of plastering you said, a skim, some sanding...'

Rob muttered, 'Aye, well, that'll be right—after they fit the new ceiling.'

Jen's voice raised in noise and pitch, 'That's just great, and where's the money going to come from, eh?'

Suddenly a little more plaster crumbled down from the ceiling, and a paper aeroplane appeared through the dust cloud. It drifted down towards the floor in a smooth, ghostly, silent glide, landing at Archie's feet. Then, another fell, spiralling silently, landing beside Jen. She glanced down at it, then up at Rob questioningly. Archie stooped down; plaster dust fell from him, forming swirls, and he wiped his hands on his dusty jeans. He picked the aeroplane up, carefully. Another small dust fall followed, and then more planes: a silent winged assault, fell on them. Archie carefully gathered some of the paper aircraft up, placing them on top of the boxes lining the room, and his dad followed suit—helping him.

Archie counted the planes, 'Six, seven, eight, nine ... Have you seen them all Dad? They're...they're like...detailed. And look, they've got sketches and patterns on them. That one, there, see, that's like the model we made; it's a Spitfire! And those, aren't they Hawker Hurricanes? I think there's four of each.'

Rob bent over and took a look, turning the aeroplanes around carefully in his hands.

Still looking at the planes, Rob turned to Jen. 'He's right you know, Jen. Look. Your room's above that floor, son, so these must've been stored under your floorboards. Hey, maybe we've hit on a bit of history here!'

Jen shook her head, 'Like your tea, then. Old and forgotten! C'mon you two—get cleaned up and let's eat.' She shook the plaster dust out of her hair and walked up the narrow hallway through the kitchen door.

Archie carefully gathered some aeroplanes up and his dad did the same. They patted down their clothes, and clouds of dried plaster formed around them. Their heads were still white with dust as they sneaked out of the room, and up the stairs, to place the planes next to Archie's models on his bedroom shelf.

'Best get back downstairs, eh? Orders are orders.' Archie's dad winked at him before giving an exaggerated salute, turning on his heel and marching out of the room and down the stairs. Archie smiled and followed his dad, turning back to look at the row of small paper fighter planes sitting lined up on his shelf, as if ready for duty.

Chapter 4

About-turn

Archie's hand fumbled as he tried his new key in the lock for the first time. It stuck. He fumbled again and turned it the other way, and it stuck again. Suddenly, the key was pulled from his grasp as the door was opened from within. Jen smiled at him from the open doorway. 'Having a spot of bother, son?'

Archie wrenched his key from the lock and stuffed it into his blazer pocket.

Jen looked at him and smiled, he smiled back, slipping his school bag off his shoulder and dumping it under the coat hooks inside the doorway.

Jen picked up the bag quickly, 'Oh no you don't, Mister! Straight up to your room. And empty out your homework, ok? How's Year nine treating you, anyway?'

Archie muttered, 'It's all right.' before gathering up his bag and dragging it up the stairs after him.

Jen watched him trudge up the stairs. 'So this is the terrible teens then?' She whispered to herself, shaking her head as she walked down the narrow hallway.

'Tea's in an hour!' She called up after Archie, turning back to the kitchen and shaking her head slowly.

Slowly, deliberately, Archie trudged up each stair, step by step, until he reached his room. He pushed the door open, slammed it shut behind him, and threw his school bag across the room onto his bed. Walking across the bare floorboards, Archie absent-mindedly drifted his hand over his model planes now hanging, dangling expectantly, from his ceiling. As if in response, they swung on their strings, poised for action. . .

Slumping onto his bed, Archie put his head in his hands and watched the planes quietly swaying. He sighed, slowly releasing his anger and frustration at. . . . Archie found it hard to pinpoint exactly what he was angry at, what exactly he was fed up with—*school, his parents, homework, school.* His thoughts were a jumbled mess. Until he looked up again at the model aeroplanes; now they were still, suspended and beautifully poised.

The aeroplanes stood for more than a hobby or a pastime to him; they stood for, somehow, easier times. They reminded him of spending time with his dad at their old kitchen table, both intent on their work. Both enjoyed the detail and crafting the small pieces into something real and beautiful. Archie stood up slowly and reached over to the paper aeroplanes which he'd laid out on a shelf above his desk. He whispered the make of the plane to himself as he selected each one, carefully. Turning them over in his hands and inspecting them, 'Spitfire, Hawker Hurricane...' He replaced each one, then picked the first Spitfire up and sat back on his bed.

'You knew your stuff, didn't you?' He said, to the unknown paper aeroplane engineer from the past.

Suddenly, Archie looked across his room. He spied ...a flight path.

There was a clear passageway between the row of boxes and his desk. A flight path, and a landing strip. He ran his finger along the shelf, stopping at a Spitfire—beautifully patterned in pencilled detail. He picked it up and held the aeroplane aloft, then paused, wondering whether he should risk flying this precious cargo. Archie thought aloud, 'You were made to fly, that's what I think. Let's see what you've got, eh?'

He pulled back his arm and threw the aeroplane, dart-like, down his chosen route. It flew straight and true. Archie let out a whoop, and air punched in a dance of victory on his way to collect it from the foot

13

of his bedroom door.

'You beauty!' he whispered, as he stooped to pick it up, and rose again, grinning and holding the delicate aeroplane gingerly in his hand. Archie looked up, across his room. Except now, at this moment, it wasn't his room—not any more. Archie blinked and looked around him. His room was transformed.

Where his computer desk had been, now stood an imposing chest of dark wooden, sturdy-looking drawers with a mirror attached to them. Archie's bed, with its grey metal frame and crumpled Star Wars duvet, was now wooden framed, with a dark wooden headboard. Blankets were folded tightly over the mattress, topped by a patchwork, knitted cover. Archie's window blinds, grey and metal, were gone, and now heavy curtains, green and flowered, framed his window. Net curtains dulled the fading light from outside, and the light inside seemed dim; it was still daytime (only just), but everything seemed... darker. Cream, flowered wallpaper now covered the walls, and a patterned but thin rug covered most of the dark wooden floorboards.

Was this even his room? Archie rubbed his hands in his hair, and pulled them away quickly, looking down at them.

His hands had oil, or grease, or something on them from his hair. He wiped his hands on his jeans except, he wasn't wearing jeans. Archie looked down to see a pair of long shorts, grey, and grey socks, and sensible black shoes.

'What the... ?'

He moved towards the drawers, and the mirror, and stared at himself. Or rather, at someone.

The reflection showed a boy, about Archie's age. But it wasn't him. Archie moved his hands over his hair and his face, pulling expressions and making sure this wasn't some kind of weird—*what? Trick? Dream?* His reflection responded: it was him, but not him. The face that looked back was rounder than Archie's. The hair was blonde, shaved short and with a greased-into-place mop on top. Archie's brown eyes were replaced by blue ones, smiley and bright – not dark and sullen. He wore a short-sleeved shirt and a tank top. A tie was draped over the side of the drawers; Archie's hand moved instinctively to the collar of his shirt, then he ran his hand once again over his face. . . over the face. . . which stared back at him.

Slowly, Archie turned away. He slumped down on the bed and looked up and around him. He noticed cardboard and paper model aeroplanes, World War Two planes, Hurricanes and Spitfires. Some were perched on top of the drawers; others poked their noses over the top of a tall, dark wooden wardrobe. He noticed more paper planes just peeking out from under the bed. They were . . . beautiful. They were. . . Archie picked a paper aeroplane up and studied it; they were the same! The same as the ghostly aeroplanes which had fluttered down from the ceiling! But there were more, many more.

'How could I. . . ? What can. . . ?'

He shook his head. He replaced the aeroplane on top of the drawers and pinched his arm.

'Ow! Not a dream then.' He told himself, rubbing the red pinch mark on the top of his arm, and sat still, gazing around his room, this room, in wonder.

Suddenly, a woman's voice broke his stunned silence.

'Arthur? Arthur? Have you finished your homework yet?'

Archie jumped up from the bed. He slowly made his way to the door and opened it, gazing out onto a hallway with a patterned carpet runner, and walls cloaked in dark, patterned wallpaper.

'Arthur, are you listening?'

Archie looked around the room in panic. He walked back towards the bed and noticed a large leather satchel, stuffed with textbooks. It had been opened, and the leather flap had been flipped up, but the books hadn't been taken out. Archie picked up a paper aeroplane that lay perched on the opened bag. The plane was half-decorated and a pencil lay on the bed—a work of art in progress. Archie picked up the aeroplane and carefully placed it at the side of the bag. Quickly, he pulled out the first few exercise books he could grab, and read their covers: 'Arthur James Dennison, Mathematics; Arthur James Dennison, Grammar'. Next, he pulled out a small, hard-backed poetry book.

The voice called again, 'I'm warning you, young man!' And steps began to thump up the stairs in his direction.

Desperate to avoid being confronted by the owner of the voice, Archie called out.

'Yes, all right!'

The steps halted.

'Right then. Ten minutes and you'll be down for tea.'

The steps, and the voice, retreated back down the stairs, and Archie breathed a sigh of relief.

Archie picked up the satchel and emptied the books onto his bed, onto 'the' bed. Their covers were clearly labelled: Mathematics, Grammar, and a small, hardback book of poems. Nothing startlingly different from his school books. Except, when he opened them, lots of things were different.

These books were neat, really neat, and the completed pages were full of work, detailed work, and lots of it, all of it ticked. Pages packed with work; completed exercises. Archie flicked through the Mathematics book and stopped dead in his tracks. His finger traced the heading of the last piece of work and the date; his finger stopped. 'The 29th of September 1941.' Archie said the date out loud as if to confirm to himself. 'This has to be a joke.' But Archie heard the doubt in his own voice.

He took a deep breath and closed the book, subconsciously picking up the paper aeroplane from the bed, holding it and turning it over in his hands, gazing at it as he did so. His brow furrowed as thoughts tumbled around inside his head. Maybe this 'Arthur' was taking part in some kind of 'reliving history' project at school, like a visit to how certain subjects were taught in the past... some mad 'school of the past' scheme? Or... this was one of those telly programmes, like when families pretend to live in a different time! That was it! But then, why was he here? And why did he not look like himself in the mirror? And why... questions whirred around Archie's head.

He picked up the Grammar exercise book and flicked through the dates heading the tasks: 4th of September 1941; he worked his way through the month: the 16th of September 1941. And the last date was... the 29th of September, 1941.

Archie slowly turned the books over and looked at the same name on the front of each one, hands shaking, breathing quickly. 'Arthur Dennison'. Then he glanced up at the aeroplanes, and a realisation began to form in his head.

'I flew the plane; the plane landed. I picked it up, and I landed; I landed—here, now.'

'Arthur Dennison, get down here now before I give your tea to the cat!'

The voice returned and broke through his startled daze. Archie rose slowly from the bed, crossed the room, opened the bedroom door and began to walk slowly down the stairs.

Chapter 5

Table for Three

Archie's feet found their own, slow, rhythm ... he traced the thick patterned wallpaper lining the walls and ran his hand down a chunky, dark, wooden bannister. These were his stairs, in his new house—the layout was the same: four stairs, then the small square landing, a turn. The rest of the staircase led steeply down to the small hall: the same, yet so different.

As he reached the bottom of the staircase, Archie tripped; something rolled under his shiny black shoe and he stumbled to save himself from falling in a heap. He reached down and picked up a small doll, made from rags and pieces of material, a tired and shabby-looking rag doll. He walked slowly with the doll in his hand and pushed open the dining room door.

Suddenly, a small girl popped up from under a heavy, dark wood dining table. She dashed across the room, lunged at Archie, and grabbed the doll out of his hands. A large tabby cat lounging on a small armchair raised its head and slowly stretched. It jumped down from the chair and walked towards Archie in measured slow steps. Archie stared down at it, and the cat streaked past his legs and darted out of the room.

'Arthur stole my Daisy doll!' the girl cried out. She was a blur of long brown plaits and a pale blue flowered dress. As she ran back across the room and plunged onto the small, dark green sofa, hugging her doll, shooting a mock angry glare at Archie. Then her face broke into a wide grin and she laughed, dancing her doll on her knee.

'Shush, you little troublemaker.' A woman walked through the door and walked up to the girl, wagging her finger, then she playfully tugged on the girl's plaits. The small girl hugged her fiercely, laughing, and returned to dancing her doll across the couch.

Archie stood staring, frozen on the spot. His eyes soaked in every detail of the scene: his surroundings, the girl, the woman. He gazed around him at his dining room, their dining room, this room. . . . Again, the size was the same. The shape was the same, yet it was so different. Music played softly from a large, wooden, antique-style radio, sitting on a wooden cabinet, at the side of the room. The floorboards were dark, but mostly covered by a large rug. A small, dark, solid-looking wooden dining table and four chairs took pride of place in the middle of the room, and a sofa and chair lined the far wall. *The room looked like...* he thought quickly to himself, *like a museum display*; he'd seen one on a trip with the school. Except that in the museum's rooms, dummies played the roles of people, and the dummies didn't move, and they didn't speak. Archie continued to look around and stare until a voice cut into his thoughts again.

'Arthur, Arthur! What on earth is wrong? You look like you've seen a ghost!' The woman walked towards him and her blue-grey eyes looked quizically into his. She wore an apron over a flowered, flared dress, and a pair of blue, flat slippers and her hair fell into small, dark, sausage curls, but it was scraped back from her pretty, flushed face. Arthur stared again; she looked like the women on the wartime history posters he had seen at school, like the dummy in that museum. But this was no museum or school classroom.

He realised the woman and the girl were staring at him, and they looked at each other; the small girl shrugged her shoulders and raised her eyes to the ceiling, and the woman looked back at him. Arthur knew he had to say something; he had to do—something.

'I think, I mean, I don't. I don't think...'

'Now, if you're going to say you're not hungry young man, I'm definitely going to get the doctor!'

The small girl laughed and the woman shoved him playfully and winked, then walked back through the door towards the kitchen, turning to call back...

'Lou, can you start laying the table, please? Ask your brother to help, once he's snapped out of his daydream!'

Lou, Archie thought. The little girl was Lou. And whoever Arthur was, he was her big brother. And that woman, the housewife wartime poster person, was their mother. Lou started grabbing knives and forks from a drawer in the cabinet, the one the radio stood on, grasping the chunky, large cutlery in her small hands, clattering it noisily. Instinctively, Archie moved towards her—seeing the danger of uncontrolled small hands and potentially sharp knives unravelling before him. He took the cutlery from the girl, who smiled up at him and danced towards the table. Archie looked down at the knives, forks and spoons in his hands. He counted out three of each, and reached into the cabinet to pull out a fourth set, then walked towards the table and began to lay out a place at each chair.

'Silly Arthur. What's wrong with you tonight?' Lou picked the cutlery from his hands and placed one knife, one fork and one spoon back into the bureau. As she did so, Maggie, Lou's mother, returned with a casserole dish pouring out steam. She placed it on

24

a stand, in the middle of the table. Archie realised he was hungry, and his stomach growled despite himself. Maggie turned and smiled, 'Were we expecting company then?'

Arthur looked at the table, three places, three people; he realised he'd automatically set a place for a dad.

'Archie forgot that dad's away fighting the Nasties!'

Archie had walked up to one of the four chairs and was pulling it out. He stopped, mid-action, and stared, open-mouthed at Lou.

'You mean the Nazis, don't you?' He asked, quietly. 'Hitler, Germany... World War Two? We learnt about that...'

'Yes, Arthur, but that's not a meal-time conversation, sweetheart.' Maggie placed a hand on his shoulder, and smiled down at him, kindly. She had cut in quickly, deliberately, and now changed the subject.

'So, young man. What did you learn at school today?'

Maggie delved into the pot of steaming, and what seemed mostly to be potato, stew and dished a heap onto Archie's plate. She piled casserole onto his plate; it smelled of Sunday dinner vegetables and gravy, and Maggie then served Lou, then herself.

'Arthur?' Maggie looked at him.

'Oh, erm, we errr, well. . . ' Archie remembered the titles on the exercise book in the school bag upstairs. 'History, Grammar, Maths. . . Mathematics.'

The music continued to play, a 'big band' sound, Archie recognised the song from an X Factor war-time-themed night he'd watched; he tapped his foot despite himself to the catchy, cheery tunes, but in the back of his mind, Archie began to put pieces of this fantastical, unbelievable, puzzle together.

Maggie chatted to Lou, and they began to sing the song together, joining in with the chorus. Lou picked her rag doll up and danced it beside her plate in time to the music. Maggie asked her to put it away until after tea. . . Archie listened, ate, and joined in now and again with an occasional smile or, 'hmmmph' as a reply. Maggie and Lou rolled their eyes at each other and smiled, and Archie continued in his role. . .

They saw him as Arthur, but he wasn't. He was himself—but how could he get back? When would he leave this, this other world? And how?

Chapter 6

Eat, Sleep, Return...

Later, in his room... in Arthur's room, Archie sat on the bed wringing his hands and trying to stay calm. He had eaten tea with Maggie and Lou with a lurching stomach and he had managed, he thought, to reply to questions in appropriate places, and to act like a normal person would, eating tea on a normal day. But nothing about this situation was 'normal'... nothing.

After tea, Archie had been persuaded to play some board games with Lou, whilst Maggie sat in the small armchair, smiling down as she fell into a rhythmic 'click, click, clicking' pattern of knitting. Snakes and Ladders, Ludo... Archie remembered playing these games with his mam and dad; they used to take a travelling set of games on holiday to the caravan in

Berwick. The games were familiar. He found himself drawn in, protesting as Lou had repeatedly tried to skip places and cheat.

Now, however, he had time to think. He had time to consider this insane, impossible situation.

Archie turned over events in his head whilst sitting on the hard mattress, in the dimly lit room. He reached down and carefully picked up the half-finished paper aeroplane. He'd placed it back on top of the school bag, at the end of the bed. Archie held the paper Spitfire in his hands, feeling its weight, its shape and again, marvelling at the skills of its maker. He felt its calming influence, and he thought again about this weird twist of events.

Somehow, in some way, he had landed in Arthur's life. And Arthur's life wasn't in Archie's time, not by a long stretch. He'd learned enough at school, and seen documentaries with his dad: he knew what time he was in—the furniture, the radio news broadcasts, how Maggie and Lou were dressed. . . This was wartime Britain: like in one of those old, black-and-white films. But this wasn't a film.

Archie had changed into starched, rough-feeling pyjamas. He was tired, really tired. In spite of himself, he felt exhausted. 'Pyjamas it is then. . . ' He'd muttered as he changed, shaking his head, he had no choice but to resign himself to playing the role of 'Arthur'. Somewhere in his thoughts, Archie felt that maybe getting into bed, falling asleep, and blacking out the situation might 'wake' him from what was happening.

Glancing again at the skilfully crafted aeroplanes, Archie had a thought. He had pulled back the stiff covers and was halfway through fighting his way into pulling back the layers of blankets when he stopped mid-action. 'Fly an aeroplane, you idiot!' Archie threw his hands up in exasperation at himself. Why hadn't he thought of it sooner? Flying one of Arthur's aeroplanes had got him into this. . . this place, or time, so surely the reverse could work. He picked up a beautifully decorated Spitfire which was resting on the top of the drawers amongst its fellow squadron members.

Planning a straight flight patch across Arthur's bedroom floor, Archie stood up. He took a deep breath and threw the plane. It flew fantastically, straight, true and quick. It landed. Archie shut his eyes and opened them. Nothing. Nothing had changed. He ran to the little aeroplane and picked it up, shutting his eyes again, and opening them. Nothing. He was still there, here—still not home; not his home, and not in his time. His shoulders dropped and let the small craft flutter out of his hand. Archie walked slowly to the bed; he was exhausted.

His mind ached; he spun ideas and theories; conjuring up possible different ways that would help him return. . . back to his world, to his time. Reluctantly, he pulled back the layers of heavy blankets and crawled into this hard, strange bed. Archie's mind re-played the scene of his journey to this place over and over again; he yawned, and started, once more, re-playing events in his head.

Archie spoke quietly to himself, trying to make some sense of what had happened. 'I picked up the aeroplane, one of the batch that came down from under the floorboards, which must've been made... now. Now, which really is, back then. And then I was taken here: this place, my house, my new house, but in the... in the past. Lou talking about the Nazis, and the dates on Arthur's school books. The early 1940s. I'm in... what did they call it at that museum? "Wartime Britain". That's where I am...' Archie's head ached and his eyes fluttered shut, despite his whizzing, active mind. His thoughts drifted to old war films; Spitfires in flight, bombers and air battles... And he drifted into a fitful, dream-filled sleep.

Chapter 7

Missing in Action

In what seemed like a moment later, Archie was wide
awake. He was sitting down, in his own school uniform: sweatshirt, grey trousers, black trainers. He
looked down and ran his hand over his trousers and
shoes, then felt his sweatshirt—reassuring himself that
he was, well...himself. He looked around his room;
Archie's eyes widened and he leapt up from bed. He
ran to a small mirror resting against a set of drawers
beside his desk and looked at the reflection—he was
back! He was, Archie. Dark hair, dark eyes, same
face; Archie felt his face, pulled at his hair, and grimaced at himself in the mirror. He was himself.

Slowly, he sat back down on the bed. Archie
reached down, picked his mobile phone up from the
floor, and checked the date and time. He pressed

buttons, frantically, checking it was still working. It was. And, weirdly, no time had passed since he'd been 'away'. None. It was exactly the same day, even the same time, as when he'd thrown that aeroplane and ended up back then.

Had it been a dream? But, when had he fallen asleep? He had been wide awake; he just threw the plane and then...

Suddenly, Archie jumped up. 'There'll be one missing!' He declared to himself. 'If none are missing, I didn't go and it was just... a daydream.' Archie went quickly to the queue of aeroplanes sitting innocently on the shelf. He knew each one individually and admired the way each was sharp, and shaped and designed—a mini replica of a specific World War II aircraft. But before he even reached the shelf, Archie saw the empty space. The first aeroplane in the neatly lined up squadron was gone. The one he'd flown across the room.

'I flew it down here. Of course! It'll be down on the floor, you idiot!' Archie scolded himself as he jumped up and walked across the room to his door. His eyes scanned the floor, but there was nothing. No piece of paper, no aeroplane, nothing. Archie bent down and looked under the door; he pulled out two boxes which lined the wall beside the door and hunted. But he found nothing.

Slowly, he walked back to his bed, shaking his head. 'It just can't be,' he muttered. 'It just can't have happened.' He stopped and turned back to the shelf. Each aeroplane now seemed to be waiting eagerly for its flight. He picked up the next one in line and held it as if he was going to fly it. 'Oh no you don't,' he whispered. Archie placed the aeroplane carefully back on the shelf and walked slowly to his door. 'Not yet, anyway.' Archie opened his bedroom door and looked back one more time at the shelf, then his feet carried him thundering down the stairs.

He grabbed his coat off a hook in the hallway and shouted to his mother, who was clattering noisily in the kitchen.

'I'm off out, Mam!'

Jen poked her head around the kitchen door, 'Where you dashing off to then? To Cameron's no doubt? Don't make a pest of yourself, Archie. Have you got any homework?'

Archie turned back, 'No, no homework and no, I'm not going to Cameron's; I'm off to the library. Won't be long.' Archie opened the front door; it clashed shut behind him and he was gone.

Jen opened the kitchen door wide and stood frozen to the spot. 'The library?' She called after him. She knew he'd gone, and her question was more one of wonder and amazement than one requiring a reply. 'The library?' Jen repeated. She wandered back into the kitchen and took a sip of her coffee which awaited her on the small breakfast bar. 'Aye, and I'm the

Queen of Sheba. The library... what's he up to?' She stared down the hallway, eyes narrowed, shook her head and returned to clearing up, banging pots, pans and plates more loudly now, interrupting the clashes with mutterings about her son's mysterious exit.

Chapter 8

Miracle

*B*ang, bang, bang! Archie jumped upright; his bedroom door was under assault.

'Archie! I won't shout again...Up!' His mam's voice rang through the air, and he jumped out of bed. He looked down at himself: tee shirt and jogging pants. Good. He felt his bedclothes and ran his hand over his pillow: no heavy, suffocating blankets. His bed was metal framed, and his room—he looked around quickly, was his room. His room, and his time. So...he was safe to sleep in his time and would wake, in his time. He breathed out a slow sigh of relief and smiled.

'Your breakfast's going in the bin if you're not down here, in your uniform, in three minutes!'

Archie smiled again, despite himself, and dashed around his room, scooping up his uniform. He stopped to stare in the mirror of his wardrobe: dark, tousled hair, dark brown eyes, pale, with not a freckle in sight. *Yes!* He smiled at his reflection and realised for the first time, he never smiled in the mirror. His face looked younger. He laughed quickly, pulled on his clothes, grabbed his school bag from the floor, and thundered down the stairs.

'Morning, Mam!' Archie patted his mam on the shoulder, gave her a quick hug, then rushed to the breakfast bar in the small kitchen and pulled up a stool. Jen was at the kitchen bench, buttering toast. Her knife froze mid-action, and she half-turned to stare at her son. Any affection nowadays was forced out of him, begrudgingly given. Jen smiled, slightly stunned at the change in this animated version of her sullen teenage son. A newspaper, his dad's, lay discarded on the bench top. Archie picked it up, stared at the date, and began to read the news stories, smiling to himself. He picked up a steaming mug of tea, his mug... Darth Vader stared back at him reassuringly from the surface of the Star Wars mug. He smiled up at Jen, who handed him a plate piled with buttered toast. She smiled back at him, but her eyes frowned and she looked worried.

'Are you, all right, son?' Jen stood still. She tried to remember the last time her son had hugged her voluntarily or picked a newspaper up to read, but her memory failed her and she stood staring at him, a little open-mouthed.

'Of course.' Archie munched on his toast and slurped his tea, and Jen continued to stare.

'But, you'd tell me if you weren't wouldn't you?'

'Mam, man, yes!' Archie snapped but smiled up at her. He jumped out of the stool and almost ran out of the hall. 'Got to go or I'll be late. It's History first and we're studying World War Two.'

'Since when have you been bothered about being late?' Jen asked, with a delighted laugh.

'History, eh? You like it then? Blimey; wait until I tell your dad. You actually like a subject, something that's not footie, at school?!'

Jen was shouting up the hallway after Archie, peering around the kitchen door, shaking her head and her voice was cut off by the bang of the front door, as Archie raced out, school bag slung over one shoulder, shouting a hasty, 'Bye!'

Jen walked slowly back into the kitchen, shaking her head and smiling.

'I'll be late... History first... Miracles will never cease.' Jen started to stack the dishwasher. She straightened up and stared out of the kitchen window, smiling to herself, still shaking her head.

Chapter 9

Historic Behaviour

Posters stared down at Archie from a pale, duck-egg green, school wall. 'Wartime Britain and the Homefront'. He gazed up at each one, noticing details, noticing the posters, more than he ever had before. A woman, a fair-haired version of Maggie, stood poised over a mixing bowl with a small girl, the spitting image of Lou, by her side. She smiled down at the girl, who was reaching up and grabbing the spoon. *'Many hands make light work'* was the slogan, Archie presumed it was about families helping each other. And cooking at home.

He looked around him; his friend, Cameron, sat next to him and mocked an exaggerated, loud yawn. The teacher was in the middle of explaining about the blackout—the dangers, and the local areas affected. Archie found himself hanging on the teacher's every word, drinking in the details. He was even scribbling notes down. He glared at his friend, who looked at him with a confused expression—mouthing the word, 'Swot,' to him.

Mr. Bowes, the History teacher, a young man in his early thirties, looked hot, and tired, and frustrated. He frowned, put down his board marker, turned away from the board and stared directly at Archie and his seating partner, Cameron.

'Look, I realise that some of you couldn't care about last week, much less eighty years ago, but you just ask in your family; some of you will have grandparents who can remember family members who fought in the war. It hit us hard here in the North East on the home front; air raids, bombed buildings,... The Germans were aiming for industrial sites, steel works, shipyards,... But, they bombed residential areas: towns, streets, houses.' The teacher looked around; some students were looking at him, and many stared at their desks or fiddled with their pens, apparently longing for the sound of the bell. He took a deep breath and sighed, trying once more to break through the walls of disinterest. 'There were nearly seven thousand people killed or badly injured by bombing raids in this region by the end of the war.' He walked up to the whiteboard, picked up a pen and wrote the number in large print on his board. 'Seven thousand...' Looking around the class, he noticed Archie, head bowed, intent on writing.

'Aaah, Archie. Can I assume you are frantically scribbling notes which reveal how enthralled you are in my lesson? Or, perhaps, you are researching games material on your phone under your desk and frantically scribbling player tips to yourself? No, I've got it...it's a game plan for your next footie game... Hmmm, what would past experience lead me to believe?'

The students in the class laughed, and Mr. Bowes walked slowly towards Archie's desk. He stood at the side of it, gingerly lifted Archie's exercise book, and read aloud to the class.

Mr. Bowes stood up and faced the class, 'Listen and learn, class, Archie's notes on Britain and the home front in World War Two which will help him fly through his History GCSE...' His voice was heavy with sarcasm.

He held the book up, with a thin smile across his mouth. The class listened and watched him, students nudged each other, smiling and laughing. He coughed, in a mock ceremonial reading.

'The blackout procedure...' He stopped abruptly and stared at Archie, and continued...'Blackout procedure: obliterate all light from buildings if possible. Penalty if light is shown—may attract bombing. Air shelters: air raid siren procedure...Bombing raids in North East; civilian casualties...'

The class fell silent and stared at Archie, who'd shrunk his head down into his sweatshirt collar and coloured deeply. Cameron turned to him again, and mouthed, 'Swot.'

Mr. Bowes stopped, put the book down slowly and the class continued to stare at Archie. Archie's teacher looked overwhelmed, and he was... speechless. He merely patted Archie on the shoulder and smiled at him, looking genuinely pleased and shocked.

Mr. Bowes leaned over and said, 'Good lad, Archie. Well done.'

The students started to cat call and jeer, but Archie smiled despite himself and felt weirdly... *what? What did he feel? Proud?* He felt proud; but also embarrassed as the class erupted into cat calls of, 'teacher's pet,' and, 'swot.'

Mr. Bowes slammed his fist on the desk. He never lost his temper, not like this. And once again, the students were stunned into silence. 'Now stop that! If you all took a leaf out of his book you'd be informed; you'd learn something... something useful and interesting. Not just how to splat the next zombie or drive a stolen car on your X Box...' He was shouting at first, then his voice trailed into a quiet, almost hissed, controlled level. But he was heard. His students stared at him. Suddenly, the bell cut through his speech, and usually, mayhem would break out. But the class waited, not sure how this controlled outburst would end.

'Just go, go on; get out.' Mr. Bowes turned back to the board and started to rub out his words. And the class left, quietly.

Archie loitered. His friend, Cameron, waited at the door, then threw his arms in the air and stamped off in disbelief.

'Mr. Bowes?' His teacher turned around, startled.

'Yes, son?'

'How could you go about, you know, looking up and researching stuff? Stuff like about our area. The families and stuff, like you were saying—about the bombings and what happened.' Archie coloured again, he was unused to having conversations with teachers, or adults, at all, really. Other than with his PE teacher, and even then, only about his footy games.

'Well, you've got the internet, obviously, but the archives and detailed records will probably be kept in your local library, Archie. Tracing your family history, like your family tree, is popular, you know? I'm sure they'd be happy to help you. So, it's grabbed your interest then, eh?' Mr. Bowes smiled broadly.

'Well, Sir, you see... Well, yes. You could say that.'

'Great, great, lad. Let me know you get on, eh?'

Archie smiled and nodded.

'Thanks, Sir.'

Archie walked out of the class, and his teacher shook his head and smiled to himself.

'Miracles will never cease!' He turned back to the board and rubbed it clean in wide sweeps, still shaking his head slowly and smiling to himself.

Chapter 10

Reconnaissance Mission

Archie narrowed his eyes and traced his finger along the computer screen. The screen showed a house, his house, but the gable end, the very end wall, was gone. It was, in fact, half a house. The librarian who had helped him and shown him how to access their archives walked towards him. 'That's it, that's your house there. What year is that newspaper from? Well done! That's an efficient piece of research. It really makes you think about the bombings, doesn't it? I mean...'

Archie nodded. He was engrossed. Usually, he was no good at talking to strangers, but Archie couldn't contain his interest, and the words came flooding out. 'It looks like half of the house just got, like, swept away. Blown clean away, but you can see—there, look, they rebuilt it. The bits you can see, it sort of looks like an open doll's house, doesn't it? See that room there, that's my bedroom. And look, it's not really been hit...or the room under it—that's our sitting room, but the rest. That's why the roof, and the bricks, they're a bit, sort of, mismatched and that's why—look. They must've rebuilt that side of the house. And that's the side that just got smashed up, look at it. It's a pile of bricks.'

The librarian scoured the screen and smiled, thrilled at Archie's level of enthusiasm. She nodded, 'Apparently the Germans were targeting the North East because of its rail links, shipyards, and steelworks. All vital to the war effort, you know? Further along the Tyne, munitions factories were aimed at, like Vickers Armstrong on Scotswood Road. But often they hit residential areas and there was so much damage. There was a lemonade factory in North Shields which got hit really badly, Wilkinson's —they were using it as an air raid shelter. May 3rd 1941, I think it was. I think over a hundred people died; what a tragedy. And sometimes houses in streets were just, like you can see, demolished, or partly demolished, like yours.'

Archie felt his old awkwardness embrace him like a familiar, but unwanted, friend. But still, the words poured out. 'I mean, we did about the London bombings and stuff in school but I didn't think we got bombed, here. And our house.'

The librarian replied, 'Oh yes, you can read autobiographies and first-hand accounts from survivors, and people who had to flee to the bomb shelters with their gas masks: whole streets and communities. Look, further down —there; that's the story about the family who lived in your house. Oh dear...' Archie peered closely at the computer screen.

He moved the mouse and brought up the newsprint, reading quickly —more eager to read than he'd ever been in his life. Almost unaware of the Librarian, now, Archie read aloud,

> 'Wednesday 22nd October 1941.
> Family killed; street in mourning.
> Tragedy struck Sanderson Terrace yesterday evening. At eight-thirty a German bomb hit and partially destroyed Number 1 of the row of terraces, tragically killing all of the occupants. Mrs. Margaret Dennison, aged 34, her twelve-year-old son, Arthur, and her daughter, Louisa, aged six, lost their lives in the impact of this vicious assault.'

Archie stopped reading and put his head in his hands. The librarian, taken aback by his reaction reached out to touch his shoulder. Archie looked up at her.

'Dead? Didn't they get the warning then? Wouldn't they be in a shelter, like you said? That's not right, is it? They would have been in the shelter, wouldn't they?'

The librarian looked at him, eyes concerned and full of sorrow. 'I'm afraid sometimes the warning was too late, or communities were just taken by surprise.'

'Do you think I could have some paper and a pen please, just to make some notes for my... school project?'

'Of course, pet. Just hold on.' The librarian busied herself, eagerly fetching paper and pen, and Archie continued to tap on the screen, studying the image, reading and re-reading the article. Quickly, the librarian placed notepaper and pen beside him. She smiled and walked away, looking back at him as she returned to the main desk. Archie began making notes, writing down dates, times, and details, and found himself completely engrossed in his task. The librarian smiled across from her desk and continued with her duties, shaking her head and sighing, wishing more young people were as dedicated to their studies as that young man.

An hour later, Archie pressed 'Exit' and shut down his computer. He stretched his shoulders and neck and tucked his paper—now filled with notes, into his coat pocket. He smiled at the librarian as he left and gave her a quick wave, which was returned. Thoughts spun frantically in his head as he walked home.

The light was starting to fade as Archie threaded his way through the terraced streets. He looked up and saw that the sky was streaked with slashes of crimson and candy-pink stripes causing it to almost glow. He looked downwards again. He realised that he rarely looked up; rarely noticed the sky or its colour. But now, as he walked, he pictured glowing red skies and flaming light—not from a winter sunset, but from German bombing raids. He could almost hear the explosions, the screaming sirens; he could picture the flames and feel the heat...

Bombs had dropped from that same sky, onto these same streets... He was lost in his thoughts, still reeling from the newspaper story about Maggie, Arthur, and Lou. And before he knew it, he was home.

He stared up at the roof of their end terrace house. In the fading light, the joint where it had been rebuilt and the original roof tiles met was just visible. He closed his eyes and pictured the newspaper image and opened them again. He could see now, where the rebuilt section adjoined the original house. It was as if a slice had been cut out of it, then piece-by-piece added back on. And the family, the people he had, what? *Met? The boy he had, become?* Killed. Killed, all of those years ago. But now, they were, somehow, part of him, his life, and his home, and... Archie felt tears brimming and burning behind his eyes. He felt sorrow welling up and tried to swallow it down. Archie wiped his eyes quickly on his sleeve, and walked to the door, putting his key in the lock. The front door banged shut behind him.

Chapter 11

Return Flight

'Tea in half an hour, Archie. Sausage hotpot. Was school okay? If you're off upstairs, get started on your homework.' Jen's voice rang out from the kitchen; she raised it over the clatter of dishes, and over the music which threaded its way out of the door from the radio.

'It was all right. I'm just going up to work on my... history project. Is my computer connected? Have we got broadband?'

Archie had started to walk up the stairs, after hanging his coat on a coat hook in the hallway. Suddenly, he turned as the kitchen door swung open and his mother stood there brandishing a ladle, which she pointed in the air as she spoke.

'You, Archie, you are telling me, that you are going upstairs now, specifically, to start something re-

51

lated to school. Something to do with learning, real learning? And did I just see you hang your coat up? Now I know something's going on...' Jen smiled and pointed at him in mock accusation with the metal ladle.

'Yes. Yes, I am, and have we got...'

'Yes! Broadband, internet, computer... and if you're using it to research history, my lad, I will eat my words. More likely Xbox-based work, I'll bet. History?' Jen stared at her son, trying to read his expression, to uncover the truth. But his face was open and earnest, and he smiled at her. Smiled, again! Jen broke off her accusations and smiled back at him.

'Mam, settle down. It's just something I'm interested in, that's all.'

'"That's all",' he says, '"That's all!" That's brilliant, that's what that is. Carry on! Carry on—don't let me stop you. Off you go.' Jen whacked him playfully with the ladle, ushering Archie upstairs. Archie smiled and pretended to defend himself, and ran off upstairs.

'Miracles never cease...' Jen whispered to herself as she returned to the kitchen.

Archie entered his room where each paper aeroplane was laid out carefully, spaced across a long bookshelf. He picked an aeroplane up, turning it in his hands, admiring it, then carefully placed it back with its comrades. 'If I can go back then maybe I can get there before, before it... and then maybe.' Archie wondered to himself out loud. As he spoke his inner thoughts, the small flickering spark of hope which had planted itself in his mind soon after he read the newspaper story in which the unthinkable had happened, began to brighten and grow.

Archie flopped down on his bed and unfolded the sheets of paper he had clutched in his hand. He had taken them out of his jacket pocket and, he now realised, he had been clutching them tightly. The paper was covered in the notes which he'd scribbled down frantically in the library. He read through the information again.

'Arthur Dennison, aged twelve...'   Evening of Wednesday 22nd October 1941. But what time? There! Eight-thirty. So, I have to try to go back. Again. Make a record of the date. And if it works, keep trying. And then, make a plan to get them all out of the house, on the remote chance I do go back on that day. No pressure then.'

Archie shook his head and placed the pieces of paper carefully under the keyboard of his computer. 'What am I waiting for?' He asked himself. He rose up off his bed and looked again at the aeroplanes. 'Which one?' Archie picked up and replaced an aeroplane from the middle of the shelf, changing his mind. The last one was a Spitfire, so... Hawker Hurricane it is. Archie picked up his precious cargo and positioned himself beside his bed, ready to launch the small craft down the length of his bedroom.

'Here goes nothing!' Archie took a deep breath, and he flew the plane. It glided swiftly and smoothly, following a straight flight path, floating across his bedroom and landing, as its shelf-mate had, beside his bedroom door.

Archie blinked.

He looked down. He saw dark, wooden floorboards. He saw smart, shiny black, laced-up shoes. His eyes followed his clothes upwards: grey, knee-length socks, just over-the-knee dark grey shorts, a woollen tank top and a white shirt. He wore a blazer and felt uncomfortable and restricted in this starched uniform. He was there, again—back then. Strangely, Archie felt a sense of... not fear, or shock, what then? He breathed deeply, looked in the mirror of the old-fashioned dressing table, and saw not himself, but, now he knew: Arthur Dennison. Relief. That was it. Unbelievably, he was relieved.

Chapter 12

Strike One

'**A**rthur Dennison! One more minute and I'll send up the troops to pester you. I'll do it; I'll send our Lou up and we'll march you to school!' Maggie's voice rang out.

Archie looked at the bed, Arthur's bed. Lying on top of the patchwork quilt was a leather satchel; the top was open and it was crammed full of exercise books. 'The date!' Archie leapt to the satchel, pulled out the exercise books, and scanned through the last entries. '24th September 1941... 24th September... 24th September... So, if I'm off to school like I think I am, and yesterday was a school day, then it's got to be the 25th of September today. And the last time it was... the 29th of September; so now I'm further away from the date. Damn. Damn it. The Spitfire got me closer, but... still, I've got to make a plan.'

Archie walked to the bed and re-packed the satchel.
'I'm coming!' he shouted out, feeling more anxious
about going to school than he had felt in his life.

Maggie replied, 'Are you awake yet? Doesn't sound
like it! We've been waiting for ages. Come on lazy
bones.' Archie looked around the room. He glanced
in the mirror and smoothed down the, already smooth,
shortly cropped hair, grabbed the satchel and walked
out of his room, and downstairs to a waiting Maggie
and Lou.

In the small hallway, Maggie grabbed him and
pretended to give him a shake, then pinched his cheek
and gave him a playful shove. 'It's a good job you're
such a handsome devil, that'll get you out of all kinds
of scrapes, young man.'

Archie blushed and mumbled a reply. He looked
down at Lou, standing with her coat on and her doll
under her arm and she smiled up at him, then stuck
her tongue out. Archie grimaced and made a face
at her, and then followed Maggie and Lou out of the
front door.

As they set off up the terraced street, Archie stared
around in amazement. People were walking on either
side of the street, and they all looked, he had to ad-
mit, smart. Women wore hats and buttoned-up coats,
and men were in suits and trilby hats—he felt like he
was on a film set. Some had children with them, and
they were dressed like him, in full uniform. All carried
satchels and wore hats and smart blazers.

Maggie nudged him, 'Right, we'll walk you to school then we're off to the high street. Unless you'd rather walk by yourself? Or did you arrange to meet Thomas?'

'No, no, I'll walk with you two. I've not arranged to meet anyone.'

Maggie raised her eyebrows, 'Oooh, we're honoured, aren't we Lou? I usually have to twist your arm to walk with us. C'mon then, we'll be late and you know how Mr. Armstrong "hates tardiness"!'

Maggie imitated a strict teacher's voice, laughed and linked Archie's arm, her other hand held Lou's. They walked up the street together, and Archie felt his stomach churn with nerves. What was school like back then, or... now? Surely school was school: stupid, dull lessons; stupid, dull teachers? He'd just have to show his face.

Tonight he'd be off to bed then... bingo, he'd close his eyes and he'd be home, home in his time. This was just like, a reconnaissance mission. He was on a 'Mission Impossible' task... except it had to be possible. It had to be.

After a ten-minute walk, they reached Arthur's school. Archie had recognised the route; lots of buildings were the same but were being used differently. There were so many smaller shops. He recognised the pubs, they were hardly different, and the names were even the same. And now, he recognised the building.

He knew it as the 'Victoria': a community and learning centre—a big, dark brick, Victorian-style imposing building with pointed grey slate roofing and small, red bricks. He'd been to a youth club on the ground floor a few times. It had always seemed quite sad, really: a big, grand building that was half-used, half-deserted. But now. Now, the schoolyard contained a swarm of uniformed boys, all feeding into the large wooden doorway with a stone, carved sign hovering proudly above it, 'Saint Christopher's Grammar School for Boys'.

'Arthur, Arthur... Come on. We'll be late!' A boy of around Archie's age, thin with red hair and a mass of freckles on his face, ran up and grabbed his arm. The boy smiled broadly at Maggie and Lou.

'Morning Thomas... Bye Archie; have a good day, you two.' Maggie stole a quick peck on Archie's cheek and he blushed whilst Thomas pushed him playfully.

Maggie and Lou turned away from the gates, and Lou turned around, straining, to make a face at the two boys.

Thomas laughed and pulled Archie along with him, towards the gaping doorway and a school day like never before.

Half an hour later, Archie realised that being at school in the 1940s was like being on a different planet.

He was sitting in a schoolroom, behind a wooden desk. The classroom was stark and bare, and wooden desks were set in regimental rows. Thomas had been glued to his side, chattering, barely noticing his short, awkward replies. He'd been thankful that his lessons seemed to be shared with Thomas, so he dutifully walked with him and sat beside him in their allocated seats.

The students looked all alike—*just like a troop of smartly turned-out small soldiers,* Archie thought. They all sat up straight and listened intently to the teacher; *like programmed schoolboy robots,* he thought to himself. Archie looked around. The class were silent, everyone staring at the teacher, who scribbled furiously on a blackboard with white chalk. Occasionally the cloaked teacher would reach behind him for a wooden blackboard rubber, stabbing at the board with it to erase a piece of his writing, and then clouds of white chalk dust danced around him, creating a ghostly image.

Archie stared at the caped figure, hovering in the white chalk dust. The teacher wore a black, flowing cloak, tied at his neck, and a black flat hat with a tassel which twitched as he swung his head around, owl-like, to peer at his students over silver-rimmed spectacles perched on the end of a beak-like nose. Suddenly, he slammed the board rubber down. Clouds of dust fumed up around him and he started to glide, Archie realised, swooping down a narrow aisle between the wooden desks, towards. . . him.

'Dennison! Where do you think you are, lad? Slouching in the sand on Whitley Bay beach? Sit up!'

Archie realised he'd slunk into his chair; he'd been nervously twiddling a pencil between his fingers and this now pinged out of his grasp and bounced off the teacher's cloak.

Quicker than a flash, Mr. Armstrong brought a long, thin, whip-like cane down across Archie's knuckles; his hand had been resting on the desk, outstretched in front of him as he'd studied the scene he found himself in. Archie drew his hand into his chest. 'What the. . . ? Did you just hit me!?' The question was shouted at Mr. Armstrong before Archie knew he was even going to ask it. He rubbed his knuckles where the tell-tale red, raised welt from the lash stroke stood out. Mr. Armstrong had turned away and was striding back to the board. He turned again, this time slowly, raising his cane, and he stalked up the aisle once more towards Archie. The rest of the students sat frozen, open-mouthed, staring at Archie, and at their teacher, then back at Archie.

Archie was beside himself with rage. He stood up, and his chair fell over backwards.

Mr. Armstrong froze, his cane arm dropped to his side.

'Get out! Mr. Smithson's office, Dennison. Now!'

'I'm going, you lunatic. Don't worry!'

Archie stormed out of the classroom, tears brimming in his eyes, and ran down the long, bare, echoing school corridor.

An hour later, he sat staring at the long, grey corridor. Silence echoed around, only interrupted by the occasional sharp tones of teachers' instructions, their voices finding escape routes through the wooden classroom doors and ringing down the corridor.

Archie squirmed and moved around in his small wooden seat, positioned outside of the Headmaster's office. The door handle rattled, and Maggie and Lou came out of the room. Maggie was ashen-faced, pale and looked, somehow, older; her eyes were red and she sniffed into a white handkerchief, embroidered with small blue flowers. Lou stared at Archie and Maggie grabbed his arm, pulling him up out of his seat. They marched back along the long, bleak hallway in silence. Archie hung his head low, whilst Lou attempted a skipping step but was pulled back by her mother. The heels of Maggie's shoes beat out a determined rhythm on the hard, tiled floor. Suddenly, Maggie stopped dead in her tracks and turned to face Archie.

Maggie stared at Archie, took a deep breath and spoke in hushed tones, aware they were still in the school hallway. 'It's because your dad's away, isn't it? You've not had enough discipline—not that he was ever very good on that side of things, mind. I'm so ashamed, Arthur. Did you hear what your headmaster said? 'There's no place for troublesome young men at Saint Christopher's Grammar School.' Troublesome, Arthur? You've never been troublesome in your life! I can't believe what you've done, I really can't.' Maggie stifled a sob and turned quickly away.

Lou stared up at Archie, her eyes were wide, and she clung to her mother's arm. Archie stared at his blackened, shiny shoes and desperately tried to think of something, anything to say to Arthur's mother. He felt... what? His stomach churned, and tears welled in his eyes. Responsible. Not angry, not any more, or outraged, just ashamed, and responsible for letting her down. But how could he possibly, even start to try to explain?

Maggie stared at him, 'At least you have the good grace to be upset.' She shook her head. 'One more chance, Arthur. One more, he said. And you're lucky to get that—just because of, what did he say again?'

'Arthur's past *elephantry* record.'

Archie looked down at her and smiled, and looked up at Maggie, who hugged Lou and smiled back at him, slowly.

'Exemplary, Lou. That means perfect, love.' Maggie looked at Archie again.

Archie shook his head, 'I'm sorry. I'm so sorry, I...'

Maggie, 'No, that's enough for now. Words won't cut the mustard, my lad. We'll just wait and see, but looking at you, I think you've been shocked back into your senses, eh?'

The three continued on their path towards the grand, double, old oak doors which towered above them, at the end of the passage. Arthur rushed to grab the handle and heaved the door open for Maggie and Lou, and Maggie smiled at him.

'That's my lad.'

The three walked out of the school grounds, quietly now, and Lou was allowed to skip and hopscotch her way down the paved streets.

Chapter 13

Sheltered

After tea that night, Archie sat in Arthur's, room. He opened a drawer in the small wooden desk, and looked through it, moving around a few items. A tin case—probably a pencil case judging by its size; some pieces of string, some sheets of newspaper. . . 'Practice paper, I'll bet.' Archie muttered to himself, and then he felt towards the back of the drawer. He pulled his hand backwards, and it held a small pile of folded-up aeroplanes. They were squashed under Arthur's desk drawer items, hidden, Archie guessed, concealing the results of his 'homework' from his mother. Archie smiled to himself and handled the aeroplanes carefully. Detailed, and patterned with pencil, they resembled the aeroplanes that had fluttered down from the crumbled ceiling. Instinctively, he looked down at his feet. The patterned rug didn't stretch to his desk; it was in the middle of the room and under his fleet were dark floorboards. Archie crouched down, bending further to peer at the floor.

Gaps. Archie ran his fingers across the floor and realised the gaps were large enough for Arthur to feed more of his hidden treasures into if he was desperate to hide the hoard from the accusing eyes of Maggie. 'Clever, Arthur my lad; very clever.' Archie straightened up, smiling still and shaking his head. He placed the aeroplanes back, carefully making sure they were where he'd pulled them from, and replaced Arthur's desk drawer items.

Suddenly, the air was invaded by the distant, muffled sound of a siren. The sound screamed louder and louder until the air vibrated with its wailing. Archie jumped to his feet, and he heard Maggie's footsteps thunder up the staircase. He realised that dusk had fallen: the scene outside his bedroom window revealed a darkened sky, and the street had come alive now, the sound of rushing footsteps and voices calling echoed around his room. Maggie burst through the bedroom door.

'Archie, why aren't you ready? Come on!' Her voice was lacking its usual, softer tones, and contained a rising note of panic. Her coat was on but pulled loosely around her shoulders, lopsided, and she had two contraptions swinging around her left arm. Gas masks. Archie recognised them from the posters they'd studied in history. This was an air raid—a warning that bombers were coming. But this wasn't the day—not this house, and not this day... He stood as if struck by lightning. 'Come on son, get your mask and we'll be off. Lou?' But before the word was out, Lou appeared at her side.

'Ready Mammy!' Lou had her coat on and fastened and under her arm, she held her cat, who hung obediently and blinked calmly at Archie. She stared at Archie, her face falling into a puzzled frown.

'Archie, come on!' Lou grabbed her mother's arm and pulled her down the stairs, taking control of the situation like a six-year-old commander, herding up her troops.

Archie jumped to attention; he scoured the room frantically. 'Gas mask, gas mask, where would you put...' His gaze flew to the wardrobe and he saw a strap, dangling down the side—the mask. It was perched on top, glaring down at him. How had he not noticed it before? Never mind. Archie perched himself on Arthur's bed, reached over and grabbed the mask, and thundered across the room and down the stairs.

In the passageway, Maggie was fastening her coat. She thrust a jacket at Archie, smiling reassuringly at them both, 'Come on you two; we know the routine by now, eh?' Archie fastened his jacket and copied Maggie—slinging his mask over his arm. Next, Maggie took the placid, lounging cat out of Lou's arms, and thrust her at Archie, passing the smaller gas mask to Lou. 'We're off.' Maggie opened the front door, and they joined the rest of their neighbours, scurrying under the howling wail of the siren.

Archie gazed up at the library building. It stood where his modern-day library stood or 'resource centre' as it was now. But it was a different building. It was grand: red brick with small, squared windows, and tall. The stone plaque above its wide wooden doors announced it as a Public Library. As they hurried towards their destination, Archie noticed the changes. His town, his area, held a mixture of modern and old buildings. The terraces were the same; time had stood still on that front, apparently. Except that none of the houses had double glazing or modern doors, and the streets weren't crowded with cars. Everything seemed, somehow, bigger. There were fewer crowds, and the shopping arcade which dominated his high street didn't exist. Small shops lined the high street; some with names proudly painted in lettering; he'd noticed an 'Ironmongers', whatever that was, a 'Cabinet makers' and a 'Grocery'. Everything was the same, but different.

People rushed up the stone steps and into the library. Archie didn't dare to query their wisdom. The library? What would make that safer, or a shelter? He'd read about public shelters—there was a huge, miles-long tunnel running from the Tyne up to Byker, a coal tunnel, used as an air raid shelter. But wasn't the point that it was underground? He followed, however, keeping his questions and concerns to himself, and they were ushered by a warden through the main doors and into the library—a grand, tall ceilinged, huge space—to doors at the side of the room, and then down some stairs. To the basement.

The light of understanding fell on Archie—this building had a huge, albeit cold and bare, basement. But it was far from bare and empty now. There were wooden benches lined along the walls, and some small wooden seats scattered around. Older people, and women with small children, were filling up the seats. Others stood around in small groups. It was cold, and people hugged themselves for warmth, looking up towards the stairway, watching the approaching feet, and legs, of more neighbours and residents.

Maggie and Lou greeted close neighbours, and Lou was offered a chair by a middle-aged man—who pushed it towards her, smiling. 'Go on, Maggie, get yourself a seat, you and the littlun' eh? You'll be all right though, big fella.' The man winked at Archie and he smiled back at him.

'Thanks, Bob.' Maggie smiled and sat down. Lou pulled on Archie's sleeve.

'Can I have Suzy please Archie?' Archie had almost forgotten he was carrying the cat; he'd been stroking Suzy's head absent-mindedly, looking around, taking in the sights. He felt like he was part of one of those old war films. He smiled down and passed the purring cat to Lou.

Maggie whispered loudly to Lou, 'You know we'll get in trouble with Mr. Wilkes the warden, if he sees her... Now keep her snuggled under your coat.' Maggie looked around, anxiously, and Lou half hid the large cat, who purred contentedly on her knee.

People were talking in hushed whispers; the warden—Archie guessed this was Mr. Wilkes, pushed the doors to the stairway closed and stood, appraising the people in the basement, and many fell silent under his stern gaze.

Suddenly, a voice rang out from the crowded room. 'It's the Gerries! They're here! They've come... they're here!' An old lady jumped up from the bench on which she was sitting. She waved a walking stick towards the ceiling, pointing and gesturing furiously with it. A middle-aged woman beside her stood up, putting her arm around her shoulders; she looked red-faced, flushed with embarrassment.

'Mam, come on, it's not them. It's the wardens checking we're all safe, down here. Sit down, Mam, look—you're frightening the bairns.' The old woman was, eventually, silenced and sat down, and her daughter looked around mouthing, 'Sorry,' to the crowded room.

A few small children, infants, were now crying loudly, being comforted by their parents, and Lou was staring up, wide-eyed at her mother. Maggie hugged her close and smiled at her; she started to quietly hum a tune Archie recognised from the radio and Lou

70

visibly relaxed and smiled up at her. Archie admired Maggie's calm, and the way she reassured Lou; she always managed to protect her from the worst of things, but without making it obvious. He realised how much effort it must take. He poked Lou in the shoulder and stuck his tongue out, making a funny face at her, and she returned the gesture, smiling. Arthur's mother looked up and smiled at him warmly; they exchanged knowing glances, and slowly, a sort of peace was restored in the room.

They sat there, Maggie humming tunes to Lou, Lou stroking the cat and Archie moving from one foot to the other, trying not to show his desperation for a seat, for an hour and then another hour passed, slowly, dragging...

Then, all of a sudden, steps were heard clashing down the staircase, and the door was flung open. Another warden—in his uniform, tin hat and armband—a twin to the stern-faced Mr. Wilkes, smiled broadly at the room in general.

'Right oh, people. The siren's finished. All clear. Off home with you all.'

'Form a queue at the door, please. Women and children first, and the elderly. Thank you. Excuse me Sir...' Mr. Wilkes had now positioned himself at the library exit; *he appeared to like seizing control,* Archie thought. He had the mannerisms of a strict teacher. Archie rubbed his knuckles and the back of his hand without being aware the gesture; he was reminded of his latest dealings with a power-happy bully.

Maggie nudged him, 'You're lucky you're still classed as a young 'un... you'd be here 'til the cows came home if not.' Archie smiled and they took their place in line, filing up the stairs, through the echoing library, and out into the darkened streets.

'Remember your black-out procedures, please! Nothing changes from the usual. I'll be patrolling to check...'

Maggie looked at Archie and rolled her eyes as the sharp tones of Mr. Wilkins were drowned in the distance. They marched along the bustling street—people were eager to get back to their own homes to escape the chill of the basement, and the evening air.

Later, Archie lay in Arthur's bed. His stiff, starched pyjamas with buttons which fastened up to his neck felt like they were choking him. He loosened his two top buttons, feeling rebellious. *Rebellious, about unloosening top buttons;* Archie shook his head and smiled. He was, he realised, getting used to things here, in this time. *What things?* He tried to work out his own thoughts. He thought back to the air raid shelter, today. The young people didn't even expect seats. And he could see them helping out in their families, looking after smaller children, helping with grandparents. *Families* seemed closer. *Why?* He lay, staring at the ceiling, his brow furrowed and lined as he tried to work it out. *No telly. No computers. No mobile phones.* He raised his eyebrows and nodded to himself. He had to confess that he missed lots of things about 'his' time. Things he took for granted: getting lifts in the car, his football, his computer games. . .

He missed all that stuff; he definitely did. You had to listen to the radio, or music, or. . . talk. Play board games. Stuff like that. He smiled as he imagined suggesting to his mam and dad that they played a game of snakes and ladders and listened to the radio all night. Firstly, they'd be in shock that he'd emerged from his room, voluntarily. And secondly, any time he was downstairs, they all sat glued to the telly, grunting out the occasional comment about what they were watching.

Suddenly, Archie's thoughts were interrupted. He heard a tapping at his door. He sat up, and the door slowly opened. In the half-light, Lou's head appeared around the door, but it seemed misshapen, disfigured. 'What the?' Archie shot up and then Lou danced across the room—wearing her long nightie and a Mickey Mouse-shaped gas mask on her face. She clown danced in front of him, then pulled the mask off, laughing. 'Ha, ha! You nearly died, our Archie! Did I give you a shock?' She giggled and bent over double at her joke.

'No, no. . . I just. . . . All right. Yes, I got a shock. Happy? You little monkey.' Archie dived out of bed and pretended to run after her, but Lou skipped out of the room, gas mask over her arm, still giggling.

'Night, night, scaredy cat!' She skipped out of the room and shut the door gently behind her. Archie smiled and rubbed his hand through his hair. He sat down on the bed, fell back and pulled the covers and top bedspread over himself. Still smiling to himself, he drifted off to sleep.

Chapter 14

Alien Abduction

Fading sunlight poured in through the gap between Archie's half-shut metal blinds, forming a corridor of striped light, stretching across his floor. Archie kneeled on his bed and looked out of the window. The lowering sunlight glinted off the parked cars' windscreens. He turned back, sat on his bed and looked down at the uniform he was wearing. He'd always hated it, but now, it seemed to him hardly a uniform at all. A sweatshirt, school trousers, black trainers. Archie moved his feet in his trainers and stared down at them, mentally comparing them to the stiff, polished, black laced-up shoes Arthur had to wear. And the sweatshirt seemed loose and comfortable, compared to the white, starched shirt, with its stiff collar and knotted tie which had wrapped around his throat. He'd had to try to stop himself wrenching his collar free, and pulling at his tie. Then a woollen tank top, and a blazer. Now, he smiled down at himself in his school clothes—*hardly a uniform at all.*

He reached across and pulled a lined notebook away from the side of his computer desk. A pen was hooked in the top of it, trapped under hoops of wire, and he pulled it free. Archie spoke out loud to himself and wrote down his thoughts, trying to add a stamp of logic to the insane events of the last few days.

'Facts: I fly a paper aeroplane which was made in the 1940s by a boy in this house. It lands. I'm transported back in time. I become him and live his life.'

Archie put the notepad on his lap, put the pen down beside him and laughed. 'Even I'd call myself a liar if I didn't know.' He shook his head and took up the notepad and pen once more, adopting a strict, clipping tone. 'Keep calm and carry on, lad.'

He continued to narrate his own writing: 'Dates that I 'land' in Archie's time: varied. Seem to depend on which aeroplane is flown. Might go back to the date on which the aeroplane was made?'

'Bedtime back then: go to bed, fall asleep, and end up back home. No time has passed from when I've crossed over. No, that sounds weird.' Archie crossed out the phrase. '. . . from when I've 'time travelled'.'

'Much better: that's not weird at all!' Archie smiled to himself and shook his head.

Archie put the pen to his mouth and then pointed to the air with it. 'But what I need to do is to be able get back there on the date of the bombing. October the 22nd. And then make a plan to get the family out. And just hope I'm in time on that date, or else...'

Shaking his head, Archie thought again, and wrote, and spoke his thoughts out loud, as if to confirm they were there, and that this was happening.

'Need to work out how to get back at the right date... Just have to hope Arthur made a plane on that day, otherwise... No good thinking about the 'otherwise'. Possible that the planes might have been made in batches.' Archie scribbled his notes down, then waved his pen in the air and spoke his idea out loud... 'Like me and Dad when we made our models! We'd go through phases to try to get them spot on, say, the Hurricanes, then move on to Spitfires after we'd done a few... That's a theory, anyway.' Archie returned to frantically scribbling his notes: speaking his words as he wrote. 'Need to work out which plane takes me back when, and keep a record.' Archie put the pen down slowly and stared at the notepad. His eyes suddenly brimmed with unwelcome tears. He was responsible, he thought, for this family's lives. *Why? Why him?* He'd not really been responsible for, well, for anything. He rubbed at his eyes, angry with himself. 'That's not going to help them.' He stared sternly at the notepad, as if willing it to hatch a brilliant plan.

He began to doodle a moon, on the side of his page. And underneath it, a cat—and an owl. *The Owl and the Pussycat.* He smiled to himself—Maggie read that book to Lou, it seemed, nightly. She loved it and knew the whole poem by heart.

Archie started to put patterns on the cat, and whilst his mind searched for a life-saving, clever plan, he began transforming it to look like Suzy, and he added to the scene. He admired his pen work—he liked art. He'd just never really tried, like in a lot of things. But... His pencil froze as he stared at the scene; he'd added some trees and a small pencil fig-ure—like Lou.

'That's it! That's it! A moonlight adventure, like in the book, taking Suzy! We could go to look for an owl for Suzy! And if we went to the park, I could leave a note and Maggie, she'd follow and search and—that's it!'

Archie flipped to a new page and began to scrib-ble notes furiously—a list was formed, and a plan of action: Archie had a rescue plan. First, he made a ta-ble. A list of dates of each flight, which aeroplane he'd flown, and the date he had landed. His eyes narrowed in concentration as he remembered the dates. Archie used his wall calendar, World War II fighter aero-planes, to mark out his flight dates and to help him compile his list. He flicked through the images after he'd charted each visit: date and time of leaving this life; date and time of landing in Arthur's life... Archie smiled and shook his head, then returned to his work.

Next, his plan. The moonlight adventure... He was still writing, wrinkles of concentration were etched across his forehead, when a rap on his door made him jump. His dad's voice rang out, 'Hello in there! Your mam's asking if you're doing your homework?' Rob opened the door and glared, mocking a stern look.

'Dad, man, you nearly gave me a heart attack!' Archie put his notepad down and stood up to face his dad.

Archie's dad wandered into his room and looked around. The room was tidier than usual, tidier than his dad had ever seen. He raised his eyebrows and whistled. 'You off to join the army, then? Is that what this is about?' He walked to the bed, neatly made, and gestured at neat piles of school books, and clothes folded at the bottom of his bed.

'I just...'

'So you've kept them all then? Great stuff. I thought there were more, mind? Didn't we count, never mind. I'm just glad you appreciate them, son. They're a bit special, aren't they?' His dad walked towards his shelf where the regiment of remaining paper aeroplanes sat neatly—each seemed to Archie to be patiently awaiting its turn at the attempted rescue mission. Rob reached and selected the first plane in the line-up. Archie froze; the moment seemed suspended in time, as his dad reached into the air, held his arm up high, and flew the aeroplane across his room.

Archie shouted out, unaware of the urgency in his voice, 'Dad, no!' He leapt across the room and attempted to catch the aeroplane, but it glided purposefully and smoothly to its landing place, just beneath the door. Archie stood still, frozen in his tracks. He stared at the landed aeroplane, closed his eyes and quickly opened them to...normality. His time. It hadn't happened! His dad had flown it, but they were still here.

Rob walked slowly towards him, smiling but looking taken aback. 'What's wrong with you, then? They were meant to be flown, son, you know? And I am an experienced pilot—as I think you'll remember?' He smiled and pushed at Archie's shoulder. Archie smiled back at him and stooped down to pick up the paper aeroplane. He cradled it as if it were a priceless treasure, walked towards his shelf, and put it in its place. Carefully counting the rest of the planes.

Rob exhaled and shook his head, running his hand through his messy mop of cropped dark hair. 'I have to say, Archie lad, I never thought I'd see the day. I've not seen you be so careful with, well, anything, really! Not even with your precious X Box games or your phone, nowt!' He was smiling at Archie and he cupped his hands to his mouth.

'Beam me up, Scottie. I've discovered an alien life form!' he laughed. 'Aha, that's it, isn't it? Alien abduction. He cupped his hands to his mouth again.

'What have you lot done with our son? Where's the real Archie?'

'All right, I've got the message.' Archie began to walk out of the room, reaching for the door handle—he looked back and laughed as his father continued acting out the scene.

'Second thoughts, you can keep him and we'll keep this one.' He pushed Archie playfully and followed him out of the room, looking back over his shoulder at the shelf of paper aeroplanes, each perched at even spaces, facing in the same direction across the shelf. He shook his head, smiling, and pulled the door shut behind him.

Chapter 15

War Games

The bedroom was dim, blinding white lights flashed furiously and the sound of machine gun fire ricocheted around the four walls.

Archie's friend sat poised on the bed; he manipulated the computer game controls quickly, skilfully, and in front of them a computer screen revealed the scene of a shoot-out in a deserted set of farm buildings—Nazi soldiers battled against British troops. The Nazis were gaining control, as British soldiers were shot at and killed—Cameron, Archie's friend, whooped in delight: his score escalated.

Cameron jeered at Archie, his eyes never leaving the screen, 'You're losing your touch, mate!'

Archie was staring at the screen, almost daze-like. His controls stayed motionless in his hand, and he replied, almost absent-mindedly to his friend, 'Aye, looks like the Nazis are going to win this one.'

'Suckers, ha, ha!' Cameron continued to use his control to mow down the British troops. They littered the ground of the farmstead, and Archie continued to stare at the scene. 'Howay, Archie! Put some effort in!'

Archie put down his controls and looked at Cameron. 'I don't care if I've lost—I'd still rather be on the Allies' side than survive as a Nazi.'

Cameron turned his gaze away from the screen, and Archie took advantage—he stared at the screen and began to shoot down Cameron's Nazi troops. His hand moved swiftly, and the Nazis began to fall, one by one, victims of his expert aim and shooting power.

Cameron threw his controls on the bed and stood up, staring down at Archie. 'What are you on about, the 'Allies' and. . . it's a GAME Archie! And anyway, who gives a stuff about it? It was years ago.'

Archie slowly put his controls on the bed. He stood up and tried to swallow down his rage. He'd never argued with Cameron—they never really talked about anything that important, or serious, now he came to think about it. Football, a bit of school stuff, but not important, life or death stuff. Not like this.

Archie began to reply, but he looked at Cameron's face. His friend looked shocked, puzzled, a bit upset and, mostly, confused. He could never explain to him, never. And Cameron would never understand,

Archie reached for his coat, hidden under the crumpled duvet, crisp packets and sweet papers. He found it and pulled it on.

'It was real, you know. And it wasn't just in France or Germany or whatever. It happened here. The war; it killed people from here.'

Cameron glared at him, 'Whatever. What's this then, a blinking history lesson? You off? What about our all-night gaming marathon then?!'

Archie walked to the door and put his hand on the handle. 'I'm just knackered, that's all. See you later, eh?' He opened the door and didn't look back, his emotions were welling up. He was angry at Cameron, sorry that he'd let him down, but angry at his ignorance, at his lack of caring. He was, in fact, furious. He was, he realised now, changed. Cameron hurled his words angrily and accusingly at Archie's back, as he left his room.

'It's because I was actually ahead for once, isn't it? Couldn't handle it? Run away, then, loser!' Cameron stood up; he scooped one of his strewn trainers up off the floor and hurled it—Archie jolted as the thump on Cameron's door echoed down the hallway. He ran down the stairs, not turning back, desperate to get some air and some space. Desperate to walk off his burning anger. He reached for the door latch but turned when he heard a voice in the hallway behind him.

'You off then, Archie? I thought it was a stopover. Does your mam know you're off home then?' Cameron's mum appeared, a fluffy dressing gown was belted around her middle and the sounds of the television echoed out from the lounge where she'd emerged from.

Archie, 'No, I mean yes, she'll be okay. I'm just a bit knackered. Thanks for tea and the sweets and stuff.'

Cameron's mother followed him up the hall, 'That's all right, pet. See you soon, eh? You two haven't had a fall-out have you?' She laughed, as the suggestion in the past would have seemed ridiculous, but now she sounded slightly worried. She was, Archie thought, really, really protective of Cameron. She mothered him and nagged him even more than Archie's mam did him—maybe because she was on her own. He'd never really thought about it from her point of view, but Cameron's dad had left them years ago. Archie had never even met him. He reassured her.

'No, nothing like that. Thanks again. Night.'

'See you later, son. Watch what you're doing, eh?' Cameron's mother watched Archie walk quickly, marching pace, down the street, shook her head and then closed the door, locking it behind him.

Cameron's mother walked slowly up the stairs and tapped on her son's bedroom door. She pushed it open, shoving the hurled trainer across the floor as the door opened further.

'Are you okay?' Her face was concerned as she put the question to Cameron. He had the computer controls in his hand, and his stare was fixed on the screen. But she knew his every expression, and she could read emotions on his face like a well-read map—he was angry and upset.

'I'm okay.'

'Did you two fall out?'

'A bit. He's been acting a bit weird lately.'

'Weird? How?'

Cameron put the controls down and turned to face his mother. He turned off the game, and Sue, his mother, sighed with relief as the gunshots and cries ceased.

'Like at school. He's been sucking up to all the teachers.'

'Sucking up?' Sue raised her eyebrows to further query his remark.

'Yes, like with the teachers. Like in history—he was making notes and the teacher read them out—and they were actually history notes! And he's been doing his own research on the stupid war stuff we've been studying. He even got himself all bothered about the blinking game tonight; he was prattling on about the Allies and the Nazis and the war and stuff.'

Sue stared at him in silence, then nodded. 'Yes, yes—doing extra work, studying, taking an interest in history. I can see you're right to be concerned.'

Cameron recognised the sarcasm and sighed, exasperated at his efforts of trying to explain the oddities of Archie's behaviour to her.

'You don't get it...'

'No, no, you're right. I don't. Because the worst thing that will come out of these disastrous changes is that Archie will do well in school. And after that? Maybe he'll get some training—go to college, university even. I always thought that lad was bright. And then, God forbid, he'll get a fantastic job! So yes, Cameron, you're right to be concerned because it sounds to me like your best mate has, eventually, got his head screwed on. And he's thinking about stuff other than football. I can only hope, Cameron, that whatever this strange force is that's changing your best mate into a responsible young man is catching! And that you'll get at least a bit of it!'

She very rarely got angry at Cameron—despite his, at times, appalling attitude. And lack of help around the house. And laziness at school in every subject except sport. But her frustration and anger rose to a peak now and poured out.

Cameron stared for a moment, open-mouthed. He turned away, picked up the controls, and turned the game back on. His back was turned, but she knew by

89

his posture her son was upset and angry. Stiff-backed, he was motionless as the game re-started.

Sue sighed, put one hand on her forehead and began to say something, but her voice was cut off by the drilling fire of machine guns once again, and the room was re-lit with flashes of fire. She shook her head, left his room and pulled the door firmly shut behind her. Cameron played on, intent on his game, but his face was flushed with outrage and anger. What had he done? What was their problem? He decided to forget them both and returned to mowing down allied soldiers with a new level of dedication and fury.

Chapter 16

Boys' Brigade

Sunlight crept through the gaps in Archie's blinds, falling in bright golden streaks across his bed. It fell upon the end aeroplane standing still and poised on his shelf; Archie looked at it as he sat on the end of his bed, and—once again, counted down the line... picking out each of its comrades. 'Spitfire, Spitfire, Hurricane, Hurricane...' Archie stood up.

'So if I choose a Hawker Hurricane, I've got to be close – but hopefully not that close, then I've got time to sort out a plan. Not too close. I can't pre-dict—right, stop messing about now. Just throw the blinking thing.' Archie picked up a Hurricane from the line of planes. He took a deep breath, shook his head again and threw it across the room.

He shut his eyes as it landed; he didn't know why, just that it seemed —right. He couldn't bear to open them and not be, there. He had to keep trying. Slowly Archie opened one eye, and a smile lifted the corners of his mouth, almost involuntarily. He was back, back then, back there... But as he looked down at his clothes, Archie's eyebrows raised. He was smart, very smart—as usual, and in a uniform, but not his starched school uniform. He walked to the mirror perched above Arthur's chunky, dark wood set of drawers. Smiling back at him was Arthur's image; he still jolted at that, but it felt weirdly reassuring now. He was dressed in a red and blue tank top, navy, knee length, shorts and a white shirt with his smart black school shoes and blue socks.

'What now, eh, Arthur? Have you gone and joined up?'

Archie fell into what was becoming a routine; he picked Arthur's school bag up off his bed and rummaged through his exercise books, scouring the last entries for days and dates. Friday 10th October 1941, Friday 10th October, Friday... Arthur looked at the clock, ticking steadily, on top of the drawers. 'Half past nine in the morning—so I'm guessing it's Saturday 11th October.' *I'm getting closer...* 'Eleven days before...'

He picked up a small white haversack-style bag, lying beside Arthur's school bag, and next to it lay a small, pill box-style hat. 'You've got to be kidding me, Arthur.' Archie picked up the hat, walked to the mirror, and positioned it on his head. Then he slung the haversack over his shoulder and looked in the mirror once more. He made a mock salute, then grimaced at himself. He took the hat off, tucked it under his arm and marched towards the door.

'Arthur Dennison, reporting for duty, Sir!' Archie laughed to himself as he reached for the door handle. 'Here goes, who knows what!'

Chapter 17

Top Dog

Footsteps rang out, echoing around the large hall. . . boys' feet thumped off the floorboards as around thirty boys, Archie guessed, roughly his age, some a bit older, some a bit younger, chased each other in games of 'tag'. He stood in the doorway with a boy who was dressed exactly the same, Thomas. Thomas—the boy who he'd met at the school and who was, apparently, Arthur's best friend. Thomas had dutifully called on Arthur and collected him from his house. They were all dressed the same—shorts, uniform, hats—discarded now and piled in a small hill on the floor in the corner of the hall. White haversacks were hung on coat hooks, as their owners charged around the hall, many red-faced with effort and shouting as they attempted to 'tag' their targets.

Standing in a similar uniform, a small, stocky, grey-haired man watched from the centre of the hall. He had a whistle and, occasionally, a shrill 'toot' and a hand gesture ensured that the boys did not get over-enthusiastic in their games of tag.

Suddenly, three sharp blows of the whistle brought the whole hall to a halt. Breath huffed and puffed out of the boys, but they stood to attention as best they could—some holding their sides, some a little bent over with exhaustion.

'Straighten up, lads! Sharp to it. Heads up! That's more like it. Right then—take your sides...hop to it. Thomas, Arthur—hang your bags up lads, plim-solls on...quick as you like...British bulldog in one minute prompt!'

Arthur shot a bemused glance at Thomas, who had already leapt towards the coat hooks and was hanging up his bag, and taking off his jacket. He reached under a bench, lined under the hooks, for a pair of gym shoes and Arthur followed suit, follow-ing Thomas' actions, pretending he knew the routine. Thomas nudged him, as they quickly changed their footwear. 'Ready to keep your Chief Bulldog title, eh? Reigning champion and all that.' He winked at Arthur, who stood looking bemused but grinned and nodded. He mouthed the words to himself as he trot-ted after Thomas, 'Reigning champion?'

The walls were bare, and high, and tall windows let small squares of light in. The hall was really just a big space, Archie thought as he looked around. As he'd walked along the high street with Thomas, drinking in the sights and sounds, he was still unable to escape the feeling that he was on a film set. Smartly dressed men, and women; old fashioned prams and beautiful vintage cars. Then they were there. At the town hall. The building was unchanged, and they climbed the stone steps together. But Archie realised he'd never been in it, not in his time, and he didn't know anyone who had. He was jolted back to the present, this present, this 'now', by a blast of the whistle. Archie felt a churn of panic wrestle in his stomach. He turned to Thomas and whispered to him.

'What do we have to do?'

'Eh?' Thomas's face turned to him, half smiling, but wearing a puzzled frown.

Lieutenant Crawford turned and saluted to Archie, 'Arthur Dennison, you remain our uncaptured champion. Well done, lad. Let's see if you can keep an unblotted copybook, eh?'

Archie smiled weakly at him and stood, making himself look ready, although his face betrayed that he was not quite sure for what.

'Right then lads, you know the drill. One big circle; mix yourselves up so I don't know who's where, legs apart, then the recruit whose legs the ball goes under is our first bulldog. Mix yourselves up. Ready...'

The Lieutenant waited as the boys jostled and swapped places, then formed a large circle. He stood, one hand covering his eyes. 'Go!' He flung the ball in the air, and it bounced once, twice, a third time, and then... the small, hard ball bounced twice across the circle and rolled under Archie's legs.

The Lieutenant barked out: 'Arthur is our first bulldog – there's a turn-up for the books! Be ready you lot; you know what a speedy blighter this one is!' He winked at Arthur, then made a sweeping motion for the boys to guide them towards the far end of the hall. Archie stood alone in the middle of the hall. Thomas gave him the thumbs-up sign from his place in the group. The large hall fell deathly silent, and all eyes were on Archie. Thomas gave him the thumbs-up sign again and Archie held his hand up and mouthed, 'What do I do?' However, his hands-up gesture was interpreted by the group as a signal to go. And they did.

Thirty pairs of stampeding sandshoes thundered up to Archie. He stood still, and each boy avoided him skilfully, running in wide circles around him until each boy stood 'safely' at the other side of the hall. The boys jeered at Archie, punching the air and whooping.

Lieutenant Crawford stood at the side of the hall and gave three short blasts on his whistle.

'That's very sporting of you, Mr. Dennison, to give the lads a chance. But how about you try to catch them his time, eh? You look a sad sight lad, one lonely bulldog. How about you build your pack up?' He looked at Archie, and Archie sensed the Lieutenant knew something was wrong. He winked and gave Archie the thumbs up, as Thomas had, but with a raised, questioning brow, as if asking if he was all right . . . if everything was all right. Which it wasn't. Obviously.

But Archie had listened: he was the 'bulldog' and he needed to catch the others. Message received. And just like that, Archie was on his game.

Football was his passion; he was quick. Really quick. And agile—and strong. And very quickly, Archie put all of his skills and passion for that sport into this game. He caught new recruits for his 'bulldog' team, easily. The bulldogs grew in numbers; each new 'bulldog' seized a running, passing boy and then they joined the bulldog team. Archie was exhausted, sweating, beaming. This was more like it: a team spirit, and competitiveness. These things obviously travelled over time.

Finally, three boys were left who had escaped becoming 'bulldogs'. They put their heads together and nodded. Archie realised Thomas was one of them. . . and by now, he knew that the last boy to make it through to the other side would be a champion. The whistle blew, and the final three charged.

Archie directed his bulldog troops, calling out commands: he was a natural leader, just like on the football pitch. They split and headed for the three boys, but Thomas was quick. He dodged and turned and avoided each lunge. Archie set out after him, but Thomas was too quick, even for him. He ran a victory stretch to the other side of the hall, and the whistle signalled the end of the game.

'Well done, Thomas, lad. An excellent run! Well done bulldogs: sit down and rest yourselves, lads.' Lieutenant Crawford stepped over sweating, panting, seated boys and made his way to Thomas, who beamed from ear to ear, patting him on the back.

Thomas danced over boys' legs until he reached Archie, who lay on his back, out of breath but content with his efforts.

'It's the first time you've not caught me, Arthur. Ever!' He leaned a little closer to Archie, quietly, this time, 'You did try, Arthur, didn't you? You didn't let me win?'

Archie sat up, his eyes rounded with surprise. 'Let you win?! Let you win?! Look at the state of me, Thomas! I'm worn out! There was no catching you: you're like a blinking whippet!' They laughed and Thomas punched Archie playfully in the arm.

Later, on the walk home, Thomas nudged Arthur and laughed and mimed: 'What do I do?' He mimicked Archie, 'You had me going at the start of the game, you did, for a bit, anyway...' Thomas elbowed him again and they both laughed together and broke into a run, dodging shoppers and prams skil-fully—back in the British Bulldog zone, until they parted ways. Each boy was off to tell the tale of their Boys' Brigade Bulldog game; Thomas over a victory teatime meal and Archie to a wide-eyed Lou and a slightly worried-looking Maggie. 'Our Arthur. You look worn out! Is that a bruise on your wrist? I'll bet this was another British Bulldog battle again, was it?'

'I'm fine, don't worry.' Archie reassured her and pulled up a chair to the tea table, falling a little eas-ier into their routine, into their lives. Each time, it became just a bit easier.

Chapter 18

D Day Landing

His hand chose the small, detailed, finely crafted paper aeroplane. Archie picked it up and cradled it carefully. He looked at the aeroplane, turning it in his hands, admiring the craftsmanship and care with which Arthur had made it.

'Heads, and it's you.' The other hand held a two-pence piece. Archie flipped the coin and watched as the decider of this little paper aeroplane's fate landed on his duvet. 'Heads it is!'

Archie stared at the other aeroplanes; only three remained. 'This is it. This is it; it has to be. I'm ready now... ready as I'll ever be, anyway.' Archie talked out loud, trying to convince himself that this time, surely, he'd land on the right day. 'Surely...'

Archie stood up slowly. He crossed the fingers of his left hand. His right hand reached for the paper aeroplane. Archie breathed in and flew the plane across the room in a straight, dart-like flight. It landed, and Archie realised he'd closed his eyes again.

He opened them, exhaling; he'd been holding his breath. First things first. . . he was back, again. 'Good.'

Archie wasted no time. . . he dashed across the bedroom and reached into Arthur's school satchel, frantically flicking through an exercise book and searching for the last, neatly underlined, neatly marginalised, date.

'This is it. Wednesday 22nd October, 1941. So it's today. . . and it's. . . ' Archie pulled aside a heavy, embroidered curtain '. . . tea time, by the looks of things.'

Archie looked down at the clothes he was wearing. 'School uniform: check.' He looked out of the window again, the daylight had faded and the street was cloaked in dusk. 'Tea time: check.'

He felt elated. He'd done it! All he had to do now was – Archie put his head in his hands as his stomach lurched. He felt sick with nerves, but he had to be strong. There was no choice. . . He took a deep breath in, and let a deep breath out, and stood up. All he could do was try. . . and just like that, he was on his game.

He raced across the room and thundered down the staircase. He flew into the small lounge and ran to the calendar on the wall—each day carefully crossed out, but the 22nd of October remained uncrossed.

'Is it the 22nd then? The 22nd of October? Today? Is that right, then?'

Maggie and Lou stared up at him. 'You're a right Sherlock Holmes. A clever bit of detective work that was!' Maggie winked at Lou and they both laughed. She walked over to Archie and ruffled his hair. 'Lou, I think we need to cross this day off before our Archie explodes!'

Lou rolled her eyes and hopped towards the dark wooden sideboard. She dragged open a heavy door and stood on tiptoe, rummaging until she found a pencil. She skipped back to Archie and handed it. Archie smiled at her and realised he felt flushed. His palm was sweaty as he clutched the pencil and placed a big cross over the date, realising his stomach had formed itself into a tight knot.

Maggie looked at him with a puzzled smile, 'You mean to say you spent a whole day at school and didn't write the date down once, then? What were you doing all day? Dreaming about those blinking aeroplanes, I'll bet.' She winked and nudged Archie, and he breathed a sigh of relief.

'No, I. . . I didn't, I just. . . '

'Well put the tea things out then, Sherlock—eh?' She laughed and walked out of the lounge, returning to the steaming kitchen where the clatter of pots and pans rang out, and Maggie's voice hummed one of the tunes he'd heard playing out of their radio, on more than one of his visits.

Maggie returned, carrying a folded, large square of heavy black material, swamping her arms. She pulled out a dining chair and stood on one side of the window, heaving the material towards the curtain rod. 'Yes, Arthur, some help would be lovely.' Archie had sat down at the table, still staring at the calendar—lost in his thoughts—excited at the prospect of his plan, but dreading the thought of failure. He jumped and realised that Maggie was fitting the black-out blind. He'd read about this at school and knew why it was done, but the information hadn't spelled out the struggle people had. Maggie was struggling on her own, and even with his help, it wasn't an easy job.

'Oooh, there's a big, bright full moon out there! I'm sure the warden would get that blacked out if he could!' Maggie winked playfully at Archie, Lou got up from playing with her doll beside the fire and glanced under the material and up into the sky.

Between them they managed to hook the dark, thick sheet of material up and pull down the edges, making sure that not even the tiniest spot of light would escape—an offence which would have the warden hammering on their door.

Archie jumped down and instinctively reached to Maggie, to help her down from the chair. He shocked himself at the impulse, but he felt... *what?* *Protective,* he supposed. He'd never had to feel that about his own mam—his dad was always there. Always helping. Suddenly, Archie looked down as he felt guilty. How many times had he offered to, or actually helped at home, with anything? He looked up and saw Maggie smiling at him, but her brow was wrinkled, and she looked slightly worried.

'You'd think we'd have this off to a fine art by now, wouldn't you?' She said, brightly, still looking at Archie with a slightly worried expression.

Lou ran back to her game, and Archie whispered to Maggie. 'How do you cope, with, you know, with all of this? And stay so, well, happy?'

Maggie had begun to straighten the tea things on the table; she stopped and looked up at him. 'What do you mean, son?' She asked, quietly.

Archie walked closer, pretending to help her with the knives and forks.

'You know, the war and your husb... and dad, and the danger and all that. And yet you still manage to seem...'

Maggie smiled at him, then turned to look at Lou, who was stroking Suzy, and chanting the words of *The Owl and the Pussycat* to her, tunefully, as the cat purred and stretched out on the small green armchair.

'I don't have a choice; we don't have a choice, really, son, do we?'

Arthur nodded quickly, ashamed that he'd even had to ask. He had instinctively wanted to help Maggie, and he knew that he felt the same about Lou, even after his short amount of time here. He felt responsible, and somehow he felt more ... grown up. And in that moment he understood. Maggie was strong because she had to be. And he'd try his best, and he'd make his plan work because it had to.

Maggie suddenly grabbed Archie's hand, announcing loudly. 'And you know what they say, don't you?

Archie, taken aback, was dragged across the room towards Lou—who had jumped up and was bouncing up and down on the spot, excitedly. Maggie reached towards the radio, set out on their sideboard—a tune was humming quietly out of it, and she turned the volume up.

'What do they say?' Archie called out, above the music.

In time with the song, Maggie and Lou sang out, 'Don't sit under the apple tree, with anyone else but me... No, no, no!'

Archie laughed as they both wagged their fingers in time to the music and shook their heads, then each grabbed a hand and they swung his arms backwards and forwards, jigging along to the music. 'Til I come marching home.'

The wartime tune sang out joyfully, and Archie felt himself being swept along in the moment. He mock saluted and marched around the room—taking the part of the soldier, and Maggie and Lou danced around and sang along. Archie stood for a moment, smiling at them, then sat on the arm of the sofa, tapping his hand on his knee to the music.

Maggie elbowed him playfully as she danced past, 'Come on Arthur, it's the Andrews Sisters— your favourites!'

Lou joined in Maggie's plea, 'Arthur! Come on! Come and dance with us!'

He pretended to drag his body off the arm of the sofa, then grabbed Lou and swung her round as she laughed and shrieked; Archie dumped her in the chair, then Maggie grabbed his arms and they danced around the room as Lou laughed and clapped.

Maggie smiled broadly but as he looked closer, Arthur saw tears brimming in her eyes. He swung her round quickly, like he'd seen the men do in the old films, and whirled her away from Lou. Maggie wiped her eyes quickly, and mouthed a 'Thank you.' He realised it was a song about being away from your loved one, and he realised, once again, how brave Maggie was being. And then it was Archie's turn to look away.

The music stopped, and a broadcaster with a clipped, upper-class accent, spoke out, announcing the latest news on the progress of the war. Maggie walked quickly over to the radio and turned it off.

'Tea will be getting cold with all our high jinks!' Maggie walked briskly out to the kitchen, and Arthur followed to help, offering to carry in the pot of steaming stew which was waiting to be devoured.

Later, after several snakes and ladders games, with the radio playing softly in the background, the rhythmic clicking of Maggie's knitting needles came to an abrupt halt.

'Right, Madam. Seven o'clock.' Maggie looked up and wagged a knitting needle in a mock telling-off gesture at Lou. 'Off to bed with you. Ask your big brother to read to you tonight. Mind you, I'll be up to see you shortly – nightie on, face washed!'

Lou stood up and gave a smart salute to her mother. She marched out of the room, and Suzy followed in the parade. Archie and Maggie smiled at each other.

Archie faked a yawn, 'I'm going to go up early tonight. I've got some history to read up on and a bit of mathematics to finish off.'

'Arthur, love... I know it's hard, Dad being away and, and the war, and everything...' And, you know when you keep forgetting things, like, say, getting told off at school or just bits of days, or nights?'

Archie felt colour creeping up his neck and over his face, as he remembered the confrontation with that old ghoul of a teacher. He looked down at his feet, ashamed, trying to think of something to say. *Memory loss?*

'I'm thinking that you could be forgetting things a little bit on purpose, forgetting, say, a school day or a... night at home, maybe when things are too hard you just, well, blank them out?'

Archie stared at Maggie, puzzled, but then, slowly, it dawned on him.

When he was 'being' Arthur, when he was experiencing Arthur's life, Arthur was where? In 'no man's land'? Not being there, but not being 'gone'. Blimey this was complicated. Archie was silently thankful the real Arthur reappeared and everything was all right for him, as soon as Archie went 'back to the future'. But, obviously, Arthur couldn't remember anything that happened when Archie took over as him. That must be weird! Archie felt troubled; he was causing Arthur some confusion, maybe even bother... but, he had no choice. He had no choice whatsoever.

'Arthur, Arthur; are you listening?'

Archie turned his attention to Maggie, and her worried frown and eyes creased with concern as she studied his face, searching for a response.

'But, I was just saying, it doesn't matter, love. Really. I think it could be your way of coping with, well, with everything.' Maggie caught Archie up in a tight hug, releasing him suddenly and patting at her eyes with the sleeve of her house coat.

'Mam, I'm all right. Really, I am.' Archie reached out awkwardly and patted Maggie on her shoulder.

'You're a brave soldier, son. Always have been; just like your dad, eh?' Maggie smiled and put her hands gently onto Archie's shoulders.

'But I hope, son, I really hope, you can, you know, talk to me. Let me know if it all feels too much. I know you don't like to show me you're upset, or sad. But, Arthur, promise me you won't bottle everything up?'

'I won't. I promise.'

Maggie smiled, dropped her hands to her sides and clasped them in front of her; Archie figured it was Maggie who was putting on a brave front now.

'Right, then; onwards and upwards, eh?' Maggie winked and walked purposefully away, turning to plump cushions on the small sofa; Archie saw how she dabbed her eyes again quickly, and he wished he could explain. But he couldn't. Not now, probably not ever.

Archie turned and walked out of the dining room, walking up the stairs, slowly shaking his head to himself, trying to rid himself of this feeling of guilt, he supposed. He should follow Maggie's example. She was strong and brave, and he needed to be too, for all of them.

'Night, night son,' Maggie called up the stairs and smiled to herself.

She walked into the kitchen, and the sound of running water and the clashing of pots followed Archie as he reached the door of Arthur's bedroom.

Chapter 19

A Picnic in the Park

Thirty minutes later, Archie heard Maggie's footsteps climbing the stairs, and her muffled tones as she checked on Lou and wished her a good night. Maggie knocked on the door and pushed it open slightly, not quite putting her head around, but calling softly out to Archie. 'Don't work too late, son.'

'I won't.' Archie still struggled to call her Mam. She was Arthur's mother, not his. In reality, his mam was... *Where was she? Not ever born yet!* Archie shook his head; if he thought about the details of this situation, it would, he was sure, drive him mad. So he stopped. And returned to the job at hand – the rescue mission.

Archie picked up Arthur's haversack. He walked across the bedroom, placed his hand on the door handle and took a deep breath. He checked Arthur's clock again, glancing behind him. Just after half past seven. By eight o'clock, he had to have his plan in full swing. So all was going to plan, so far. *So far. . .*

It had happened, he'd read, at half past eight. Half past eight that night. So no matter what, the house had to be empty at that time. It had to be.

North Shields Park was just a ten to fifteen-minute walk away. And he'd noticed that Maggie popped upstairs each night before the eight o'clock radio news broadcast. She would check on Lou, and knock and say goodnight to Arthur. Then she would go back downstairs, make a cup of tea and return to her knitting, and she'd listen to the news on the radio. His whole plan relied on Maggie being a creature of habit. Archie realised he was crossing his fingers, again. As he did so, he realised his palms were sweating. He wiped them on his school trousers, and he walked across the hall and opened Lou's door.

Lou was dressed in her nightgown, and she was sat up in bed—Suzy was curled in a ball beside her, purring loudly. Lou's bed was covered in a patchwork quilt, similar to Arthur's. A small wooden seat was positioned beside her bed, and a book lay ready upon it. Archie took a seat and picked up the book.

'*The Owl and the Pussycat.* What a surprise?' Archie laughed; Lou was always reciting this poem and she knew it off by heart. It was, in fact, the basis for his plan—

'Come on, Arthur—me and Suzy have been waiting for ages.

Archie opened the book and Lou leaned over, tracing her finger over the pictures. She lay back, one arm around the purring cat, and smiled up at him.

Archie began to read. He didn't read much at home, and only the essentials for school, and the book—with its pictures weaving around the words, took him back to when he was small. His dad would usually be the one reading him to sleep... As his thoughts drifted, he realised he was reading the words almost automatically. He'd heard this poem, this story, himself. *Had his dad read it to him?*

'Arthur!' Archie was jolted out of his thoughts and looked up from the book. Lou frowned and crossed her arms moodily. 'What's wrong with you Arthur? You're not even showing me the pictures and you're not reading it properly.'

'What? The picture? Oh, yes, I mean...'

'Start again please.'

Archie began the story again, this time trying to read with some meaning or, he guessed, feeling—and he pointed to the images as he read.

The Owl and the Pussy-cat went to sea,
In a beautiful pea-green boat:
They took some honey, and plenty of money,
Wrapped up in a five-pound note.

117

The Owl looked up to the stars above,

Archie looked at Lou and her eyes were drooping, but a smile lifted the corners of her mouth. Suzy purred by her side. Archie spoke up, reading louder—he needed Lou awake. He needed to tell her about the plan.

They danced by the light of the moon,
The moon,
The moon,
They danced by the light of the mooooooon!'

Lou's eyes shot open and she looked a little startled, then she laughed as Archie made a howling noise, pretending to howl at the moon. He repeated the line.

'They danced by the light of the mooooooooon!'

'Fancy a moonlight picnic, then?!' Archie cupped his hand and stage whispered this to Lou. He watched her eyes widen and a mischievous grin spread across her face.

Lou frowned, 'But what about Mam? She'll worry, Arthur... We shouldn't...'

Archie smiled. 'We'll only be gone an hour, and Mam won't even know.'

Lou's small brow furrowed as she juggled the impending adventure against a sense of worry and guilt about her mother's worries.

Archie realised more convincing was needed.

'Don't you think that our Suzy deserves a lovely adventure and a chance to find her very own owl? Eh?'

Archie picked up the purring cat and gestured to the picture in the book of the owl and the pussycat sailing off into the moonlight.

Lou's face broke into a wide grin. 'But we won't be long, will we? And Mam won't even know.'

Archie smiled back at her and nodded.

Chapter 20

The Great Escape

Archie looked at the clock, ticking away the minutes, steadily, on top of the chest of drawers. Ten to eight. It was time.

In one swift motion, he pulled on a thick woollen jumper, excavated from the bottom of one of Arthur's dresser drawers. He reached for the haversack and began to tip-tap his way across Arthur's rug-covered floorboards. He looked down at his feet—he'd changed into Arthur's gym shoes, so he could creep quietly across the floor. The floorboards creaked, but not too loudly, yet Archie still grimaced and winced at the noise. He hoped, desperately, that Maggie's knitting and the noise of the radio would engross her, and she'd not hear any commotion or movement upstairs.

He crept out of the room, up to Lou's door, and

turned the doorknob, slowly. Lou was sitting up in bed, a small table lamp was switched on beside her, and she and Suzy looked up at him.

Lou gestured a *Shhhh!* to Archie, and she stroked Suzy, who lay contentedly on the bed beside her. Lou had dressed herself quickly and quietly: a huge achievement for her, Archie realised. Archie had told her to dress warmly, and Lou had duly fastened over her nightie a chunky red cardigan. Archie grinned as he realised it was buttoned wonkily, but decided not to aim for perfection: it was thick and would keep Lou warm, and that would do. Archie had planned to quietly unhook Lou's coat from the hall coat hooks, but he gave her a thumbs up as he realised she had fished a thick winter coat from her wardrobe. Last year's he guessed, as it seemed small—but she'd managed to squeeze into it. It squashed her chunky knit cardigan into submission, and Lou wore a green, home knitted, scarf wrapped warmly around her neck. She wore thick socks and a pair of black wellingtons perched at the end of her small legs, which she dangled over the bed. Arthur smiled again at her odd socks, but, once more, decided warmth was the key.

Lou grinned at him and gestured to a large basket, ready, he assumed, to transport Suzy. Luckily, the big cat seemed to be putty in Lou's hands. He remembered smuggling the large, purring Suzy into the air raid shelter, and he was grateful for the cat's sleepy, placid nature.

Lou made as if to get out of bed, but Archie quickly sat beside her and copied her *Shhhh!* gesture, pointing downwards—making an angry face, pretending to be an angry Maggie. Lou smiled and nodded, then whispered the question again, 'What's in the bag?'

'Listen, if we want to find Suzy her own Owl, we need to keep really quiet as Mam will go mad if she finds out. Right. We're off on our... moonlight adventure. We'll take off, with Suzy, and we'll go to find her very own owl, in the park. By the light of the moooooon!'

Lou clapped her hands and bounced on the spot with excitement. ' Suzy's Owl... We'll see her Owl... and they'll dance by the light of the moooooon!' She was still whispering, but could barely contain her excitement. And Archie, though his heart was in his mouth, smiled down at his sister.

'We have to creep downstairs so that Mam can't hear us. We can put Suzy in the basket, and I'll carry her, but you stay close behind. You can bring the book and pass me the torch,' Lou picked up her book and tucked it under her arm, saluting playfully, and passed the torch carefully to Archie. 'Thanks,' he whispered, holding on to it tightly. With a loud, stage whisper, 'When we get downstairs, I'll slip this note under the kitchen door, so Mam knows we're all right. Then we'll sneak out of the door, really, really quietly. All clear?'

Lou gave a mock salute again and stood to attention, 'Yes sir!' She whispered. It took every ounce of self-control she possessed, but she stayed still, and quiet, and waited to follow. Archie helped Lou place the sleepy cat into the basket. Suzy didn't protest, she simply nestled in, with her head poking over the side. Archie clutched the haversack and the basket full of a sleepy and still purring cat and hugged it carefully under his arm. He sighed, relieved that Suzy was such a lazy and laid-back cat.

Archie then crept slowly across Lou's room, quietly, exaggerating his movements, trying to make them comical, but gesturing for Lou to copy them, which she did. They made pantomime miming gestures of *Shhhh!* to each other, and crept down the stairs. The sound of the radio, tunes—trumpets and singing, floated from the lounge, and the click, click, click of knitting needled confirmed Maggie's presence to Archie's grateful ears.

He motioned for Lou to stay still, like a statue, and she complied—smiling from ear to ear, enjoying their adventure. He slipped the note under the kitchen door, physically and mentally crossing his fingers that Maggie stuck to her nightly routine. Archie took up his position as leader of this nocturnal expedition and guided Lou down the hallway. He opened the front door slowly, quietly congratulating himself on his silence and stealth, and then they crept, cat burglar-like, out, into the dark, blacked-out streets.

Archie waited until they were out of the house, then shone the small torch to light up their way. Each household had been given one to help them to run to the bomb shelter in the blackout. Archie carefully aimed the small beam downwards, just in front of their feet, so they didn't give themselves away in the dark, terraced streets. They could only just make out their way and they both blinked as their eyes grew accustomed to the darkness. The last thing he wanted was to attract the attention of a warden; they'd be promptly marched home, no doubt.

Lou held on to Archie's jumper, and skipped along beside him, chanting the words to her favourite poem, quietly, singing the words and hopping with excitement.

Chapter 21

In Hot Pursuit

Maggie laid down her knitting needles and patted straight the piece of grey, knitted material she'd constructed. It was going to be a new jumper for Arthur—and she smiled as she realised it was taking shape nicely. She yawned and stretched, and rose from the small armchair. She picked up a photograph which was positioned in pride of place, centrally, on the sideboard. It was of herself, and a man who was dressed in a smart suit—Maggie wore a hat and a flower corsage was pinned to the lapel of her fitted jacket. Her wedding day. Fourteen and a half years ago—no thoughts of war or rationing, or Hitler or.... The smile faded as she wiped some imaginary dust from the small pane of carefully polished glass. She shook her head, and pulled her shoulders up, stretching her neck—it ached from looking down at her knitting needles. She walked slowly out of the room, mentally reproaching herself for dwelling on things, things she could do nothing about. Things. . . She stopped as she began to open the kitchen door.

Something was jammed underneath it; Maggie bent over to try to dislodge it. She smiled as she reached for the piece of paper—Arthur. A paper aeroplane, no doubt. That boy was obsessed, she was still smiling as she picked it up, but her smile faltered as she read: 'Mam'.

A note? She smiled again—a prank, no doubt.

Maggie shook her head and walked into the kitchen, her slippers flapping as she walked across the floor, unfolding the paper. She read. Suddenly, her body sagged and she held on to the bench top for support as she read aloud the words which sprang up under her eyes. The handwriting was different for Arthur—irregular, not as neat, but this fact ran from her mind as the contents of the note sank in.

She read aloud, half sobbing:

> *'Mam. Please don't be mad. I've taken Lou for a moonlight picnic, to cheer her up. We've taken treats to eat and Suzy also (to see if we can find her an Owl to run away with, like in her poem)! We are just going to the park, so please don't panic, Mam.'*

'Don't panic?! Don't panic?!' Maggie's voice level rose and she waved the note around, before forcing herself to read on. . .

> *'We will only be an hour or so, so there's no need to come and fetch us, really.'*

'No need to come and fetch us?!' Arthur Dennison, you have lost your mind! No need. . . '

Maggie walked around in circles, tears began to brim her eyes as she thought of her children walking around, in the pitch black, alone, unprotected.

Maggie began to move quickly. 'The torch.' She ran up the stairs, and into Lou's room. She knew Lou used it to read, and the small torch should have been there, on the floor, beside her bed. Maggie sobbed as she stooped to search for it, and put her hand on her daughter's empty bed, realising Arthur must have taken it for their 'adventure'.

'Oh, Arthur. How could you?' She stifled a sob, and then ran out of the room and thundered down the stairs, wiping the tears from her eyes quickly. Maggie kicked off her slippers, slipped on some shoes, and grabbed a coat from the coat hooks at the side of the small passage. She ran her fingers over her hair—it was set in large curlers, but she didn't care. She opened the front door and it slammed shut behind her, and she hurried to her neighbour's house, banging on the door and calling out loudly.

'June! June!'

Within less than a few minutes, a woman appeared. Like Maggie, June had her hair set in rollers. She wore a dressing gown and slippers and carried a copy of a newspaper in her hand. 'Maggie! What the...?'

June was Maggie's neighbour and her friend. They both had husbands at war, but June had no children at home. There was just her, and she doted on Arthur and Lou, to whom she was 'Aunty June'.

'June, I need your torch.'

June stared at her friend with curlers in her hair and she quickly glanced at her misbuttoned coat and tearstained face.

'Maggie, what...?'

'No time! No time, June! I just need...' Maggie burst into a sob, and June quickly grabbed her as she crumpled.

'It's our Arthur, June. He's gone mad. I told you he'd been acting all odd, didn't I? But this ...' Maggie sobbed and handed the note to June. June read it, quickly, and looked at Maggie, open-mouthed, then gathered her thoughts. Maggie's eyes were red and swollen, and she looked panic-stricken. June grabbed Maggie's shoulders and spoke calmly.

'Maggie, love. I know it seems mad, but your Arthur has got his wits about him. And the park is just over a ten-minute walk away. And let's face it, nobody's around after the blackout, eh? Only the warden. And he'll have them back here sharpish if he catches them, eh?' June smiled, as they both knew the Warden was a man who liked his job and relished the opportunity to play street policeman.

Maggie nodded, 'We have to go, June. We have to follow them.'

'Of course we do. Right then. I'll grab the torch and my coat and, oops, some shoes would be good eh?' She kept chatting as she got ready, staying upbeat, and calming down her friend. But as she turned to reach for her things, June's brow furrowed. This was so out of character for Maggie's son—he was so... sensible, and reliable. But there was no time to worry, not now.

Chapter 22

By the Light of the Moon

The moon spun silver threads of light across the dark silhouettes of trees which opened up into a clearing, and the grass here was bathed in the dim glow of light. Archie had folded a blanket from his bed into the haversack and he'd spread it on the ground where he, Lou and Suzy sat in the middle of their makeshift table. He'd managed to sneak out a handful of biscuits which Maggie had baked, and he spread these in the middle of the thick, woollen blanket. 'This moon is lovely, Arthur! Did you pick this night because it's big and bright? Is that why you chose tonight for our adventure, our Arthur?' Lou picked up a biscuit and crunched loudly as she ate it, crumbs sticking to the sides of her mouth.

Lou's face was tilted towards the moon and the stars, and it lit up as she looked at Archie. Archie was reading from the large, open, The Owl and Pussycat book; the torch was lighting up the words and the pictures. His stomach lurched as he thought about the real reason for picking this night, and his mind raced, desperately hoping Maggie had found his note, *otherwise...* But it was no good thinking about 'otherwise'.

'I, eh, well, yes...I did. It's amazing, isn't it?' Archie looked up at the moon. His insides were churning. He looked at the watch, Maggie's watch, he'd picked it up off the sideboard whilst she made tea and he had it stuffed in his trouser pocket. He'd felt so bad for taking it, even for this cause, but it had to be done. Arthur didn't seem to have a watch, and he needed to time this desperately important mission.

'Arthur it's all right, Mam will know we are all right, won't she? And she'll be having her cup of tea now, won't she?'

'God, I hope not.' Archie said aloud: the time was ten past eight. *Twenty minutes to go until...* Archie blocked the thought from his mind. Maggie would come for them; she had to. She should be out, looking for them, right now; he crossed his fingers and hoped, desperately, that she'd picked up his note. Lou looked at Archie.

'What did you say, Arthur?'

134

'I said I hope so, of course she will. Now, have you seen Suzy's owl yet? Maybe we need to 'Twit twooooh' one out of the trees?'

Lou began to call down any owls which were potentially lurking and ready to play their part in her bedtime story. Archie smiled at her, but his eyes scoured the rest of the park nervously. He shone the torch over the flower beds which surrounded their square of grass, up the pathway, and then, suddenly, two flickers of light appeared at the top of the pathway. Just where the wrought iron fence and gateway marked out the opening of the public park, *two lights! Torches?* The lights fluttered their way towards them, and Archie shone the torch in their direction, letting the approaching, darting, firefly-like light holders know where they were. *Two? Who would she bring? Oh, god!* He hoped it wasn't the warden, or two wardens, or...

'Arthur! Our Arthur? Lou!' Maggie's cries shattered the moonlit stillness. He smiled and breathed out a sigh. It was as if he'd been holding his breath, waiting for this moment, for a lifetime. She was here. And the house was empty. Empty, and about to be partly demolished. But he didn't care. They were here, and they were safe.

In a rush of dim torchlight, Maggie appeared, with another woman, dressed, Archie realised, almost identically. They made a strange sight—rollers bobbing in the moonlight—but Archie lost his smile as he saw the anguish on Maggie's face. She scooped Lou up and held on to her, tears streaming down her face, then Maggie placed her down, and Lou ran for a welcoming cuddle from June. Archie had stood up and he felt useless, awkward, again, guilty... and powerless. He couldn't tell Maggie why, never. He couldn't explain—he just had to take whatever was coming. Maggie stared at him and suddenly grabbed him and hugged him tightly, then she took his shoulders and shook him, but gently. 'Have you lost your mind, our Arthur? An adventure?! The warden would have your guts for garters! I swear, Arthur...'

'But the warden hasn't got him, Maggie love; we have. And they're safe and sound. And we'd all better get back home, eh? Come on pet.' June picked Lou up and Lou swung her legs around June's side, familiar and happy with being swept up by her aunty. Archie tidied up the blanket and picked Lou's book up. He carefully shook and folded the blanket and stuffed it into his bag. And Maggie bent down to scoop Suzy up and tucked the sleepy cat under her arm. 'Arthur... What on earth gave you the idea...?'

Archie shrugged his shoulder, classic 'Archie' reply, he thought, casting his eyes down and looking at his wet sandshoes.

Maggie shook her head and sniffed, wiping a hand under each eye to blot the remains of tears. 'Never mind. Time for fifty questions at home, eh?'

Archie nodded and hooked the bag onto his shoulder. Maggie linked him, her relief about her children being safe overriding her anger and disbelief at Arthur's exploits. She carried Suzy tucked under one arm, and they all headed home.

Archie felt a mixture of elation, and shame. He managed to shrink away for a moment from Maggie's arm, and looked quickly down at her watch, pulling it briefly from his pocket. Quarter past eight. They were walking at a slightly slower pace, June carrying Lou; he realised they'd get there just as it happened.

Fifteen minutes later, the foursome walked past the library, past the town hall building, and turned down a terraced street. They walked in silence, the dark pierced by their three dim torch beams. They followed the trails of light—the sound of Lou humming the tune to her favourite song was accompanied by the tapping of their footsteps, ringing out through the cloak of darkness. Suddenly, a dull rumbling shook the sky. They stopped and stared at each other.

June grabbed Maggie's sleeve, and they looked up, skywards. A light seared across the sky, and the rumbling became a dull thunder. Sirens began to wail...
screaming out their warning... and in a flash of ear-splitting noise, an explosion lit up the sky.

'It's our street...' Maggie's voice flew above their ears. She began to half run, her legs taking her home-

137

wards—June calling after her. Archie followed, then June, still carrying Lou, and suddenly...the explosions stopped. The thundering retreated into a dull hum, and the sky burned—orange, red—and fountains of smoke spiralled up into the glowing night.

Maggie ran, followed by Archie, then June with Lou running by her side, clinging on to her hand. They reached the end of their long terraced street. Neighbours had poured from their homes, some in night things—all staring at the end of the street which held their house. Two men in uniform—neither of whom Archie recognised from the neighbourhood or the air raid shelter—held rope stretched across the street and were trying to guide people to one side of the makeshift barrier.

Thick smoke swirled through the air and sparks flew from the burning end building; people shielded their eyes from the glow of the flames as they watched, helplessly. Suddenly, the rumble of an engine was heard and the crowd turned to see a fire engine, with a team of men in dark uniforms and hard hats perched upon it. With lightning speed they unravelled a long hose, and ran past the wardens, dragging the giant snake of a hosepipe with them. And soon, water began to douse the flames and dampened the showers of firework-like sparks which spluttered and hissed in response.

Archie felt himself smiling, widely, beaming; he had done it! Yes, the building was half destroyed;

yes, it was a frightening scene and yes, the family had lost their home. But they were here, alive, safe. He had, he thought to himself, changed history. He felt arms wrap around him and Maggie turned him to her, hugging him fiercely. 'You are our hero, Arthur, my lad. It's as if...' But Maggie was interrupted by June.

'Watch out, the warden's about. Look, he's waving us over people. Quick to it: a cup of tea, that's what we need. A nice hot cup of tea...'

Maggie, Lou, June and Archie pushed their way through the huddled crowd. Occasionally, Maggie and Lou were hugged by neighbours—offering lodging, supper, offering help; offering any help they could give. Arthur received the odd pat on the back or a quick hug, as word seemed to spread about their lucky escape.

Archie had never seen anything as bad as this, ever. Just on television. It was a real-life wartime drama, a bombing, and explosion, a building burning and yet... And yet, people were so: he looked around and realised, warm, and friendly, and concerned, really concerned. *What was it they called it?* 'Wartime spirit,' he remembered. Empty words on a page linked to black and white pictures of people smiling at the camera. People in old-fashioned clothes, in a black-and-white world which for him, had sprung into colour. It had sprung into an interactive, 3D, technicolour reality. And weirdly, he

139

realised, he felt... at home.

He made his way through the crowd, responding politely to pats on the shoulder and on his back, and smiles from strangers. He felt his smile return. He was proud, more proud than he'd ever been, more proud than scoring any number of winning goals—he'd achieved more than he'd ever thought possible.

Now, he needed sleep. And to get back to his home, his real home. *And then?* Proof. Confirmation that he'd managed to change the course of history for this family. And he knew how to get it.

Chapter 23

All Change

The radio fed out sounds of guitar music and they streamed from behind the kitchen door; the smell of toast cooking drifted up and was inhaled by Archie. His stomach rumbled in response, and he realised he was hungry. His feet thundered down the stairs and he barged into the kitchen and grabbed two slices of hot, buttered toast from a plate.

'Hey, mister, how about a "good morning, Mam"? Where are you dashing off to, eh?'

Jen had a cup of tea in her hand and wore a fluffy turquoise dressing gown with matching slippers. Her hair was piled in a ponytail, and she gestured at Archie accusingly with a teaspoon, held in her other hand.

'Library,' Archie replied, words muffled from a

mouthful of toast. He gave her a quick kiss on the cheek and a careful hug—wary of spilling her tea. He rushed out of the kitchen, toast in hand, and grabbed his coat from a coat hook in the hallway. He stopped, briefly, realising the position of the hooks hadn't changed. He jolted himself back to his task: proof.

Jen stood, stock still, with the teaspoon held mid-gesture, mouth slightly open. She smiled, amazed, thrilled at the brief display of affection from her ever-moody, often sullen, son. She touched the teaspoon to her cheek, then recoiled—it was still warm. And laughed at her own mistake.

'Enjoy, then!' Jen called after him. 'Make sure you put your coat...' Her plea was cut short by the slamming thud of the front door. '...on.' She shook her head and was still smiling, stirring her tea when Rob walked into the kitchen.

Rob smiled, 'Where's the fire, then? He was off like a shot, wasn't he?'

Jen nodded, turned to lift the teapot and poured a cup of tea for her husband, she passed him the cup of steaming tea. Rob's hair was ruffled, and he had a pair of paint-splattered jeans on and an old, much worn, faded black tee shirt. He took a seat at the small breakfast bar, lining the edge of the kitchen, and began to pick up a newspaper. Jen opened a biscuit barrel, and absent-mindedly passed it to Rob.

'Have you noticed, Rob, how he's been. . . different, preoccupied and, well, I don't know, polite! And just, well, different. Did you see his school report? I don't know what's happened to him. It's not bad, you know. The changes, I mean. They're all for the better, much better. . . like—have you seen his school report? I just. . . '

Rob looked up from his newspaper, 'You do know you're babbling now, don't you?'

Jen nodded, smiling, 'I know, but, what I'm trying to say is, he's like a different lad! Look. . . ' She walked to a letter rack, perched on the wide sill of a small, side window. At the front some A4 white sheets of paper stood up, held in place with a grey small cobblestone, a makeshift paperweight.

Jen picked up a pair of glasses from the kitchen bench and unfolded the report—again. The creases appeared to have been folded over a few times: the page fell open easily and showed signs of slight wear from Jen's handling the precious document, reading and re-reading.

'Right then. Let's take a subject he's never really tried in, one he always seems to have messed around in, like. . . History.'

Rob put his newspaper aside, realising that the focus of his reading was not going to be world news just yet; this news was focused more locally. He smiled at his wife, noticing the lines of concern and focus forming on her forehead as she peered at the report.

Rob gave a wry smile, 'Aye, but that could be nearly any subject.'

Jen nodded, rapidly and looked at him, waving the report in a gesture of agreement, like a lawyer who'd won an important case with a court of law legal document. 'Exactly! What was the only subject last year he got a good all-round score for? Effort, attitude and achievement?'

Rob answered quickly, 'P.E.'

Jen walked purposefully towards him, and slapped the document on the breakfast bar surface, directly in front of Rob. Triumphant in her victory.

'Well feast your eyes on this. Go on. Check out his History scores, and comments. And his Maths isn't terrible... Then what the English teacher says about his creative writing. I think I'm in a minor state of shock.'

Rob began to read, 'Blah, blah, blah... hang on, listen to this from his History teacher: "Archie has worked 'enthusiastically'; he has 'improved significantly'." Look at that! "Archie has undertaken independent study..." Independent study?'

Rob stared at Jen, then re-read the last piece of information, mouthing the words to himself, as if to confirm their presence.

Jen smiled, nodding, happy that he now shared in her amazement. 'Independent study. Our Archie!!!

What do you reckon, a visitation or alien abduction?'

Rob and Jen laughed and shook their heads, both staring at the report.

Rob put down the report, picked up his cup of tea, and selected a biscuit from the tin. Dunking it quickly, skilfully, he placed the whole, half-melted biscuit in his mouth—gesturing his cup towards Jen and saying in biscuit-muffled tones, 'Don't look a gift horse in the mouth, that's what I say. Whatever it is, let's just hope it lasts, eh?'

Jen continued her case presentation, with another string to her bow... more proof of their son's dramatic transformation. 'And, have you seen the care he takes of those paper planes upstairs, and how tidy his room is, Rob? He's been researching their types, and putting them into categories. His room is tidy, Rob, tidy— folded clothes, stuff put away. I think I'm starting to get really worried now.'

She took a seat beside Rob on the neighbouring breakfast bar stool and stared out of their kitchen window. Rob looked at her. Every thought Jen had seemed to play out across her features; she was, emotionally, an open book. He loved that about her, but it also meant he could see her worries, any stresses. And there they were—laid out, openly showing. And she was, right now, a strange mixture of elation, and concern. He put his arm around her shoulder and tilted her face towards him, gently.

Rob spoke soothingly, 'Look, love. Everything, all of the changes are, well, good... for the better, let's say—aren't they? Eh?' Jen looked at him and nodded, smiling a thin smile in agreement.

Jen turned to gaze out of the kitchen window again and spoke quietly. 'Do you know where he's gone in such a hurry?'

Rob picked up his cup and took a sip, 'No idea. But I'm guessing it's football-related?' Rob picked up his newspaper, assuming they were putting the matter to rest and Jen was, at least a little, reassured.

Jen paused, then turned to Rob. 'The Library.'

Rob put the paper down and looked at Jen, open-mouthed, and then he smiled. 'Now I know you're winding me up. We haven't even got a library any more, have we?'

Jen picked up the discarded newspaper and hit it playfully off Rob's arm. 'Shame on you! Yes, it's behind the shopping precinct. It's been knocked down and rebuilt. It's our 'Learning Resource Centre' now though.'

Rob pretended to defend himself, grabbing the newspaper from his assailant. 'Oh yes, like you would know!'

Jen smirked, smugly. 'I would know, as a matter of fact! But only because when he says he's been going there I haven't been believing him, so I kind of casually, sort of, followed him last week, being careful

I wasn't spotted. . . '

Rob's eyebrows raised, and he laughed at his wife's exploits, 'Did you wear a wig and sunglasses, then?'

Jen nudged his arm in response. 'No, seriously, though, Rob. He really went there. And settled himself down at their computers. And he was chatting to the librarian lady like he knew her. Sounds silly, really, but I got a lump in my throat.'

Rob put his arm around her shoulders and hugged her, 'You softie.'

He turned away quickly, Jen realised. She knew him. She knew he was emotional, and he was covering it up. He reached for the newspaper again, pretending to study the front page. She waited for the comment, which she knew was coming, smiling to herself.

'I stand by the alien abduction theory, myself. Keep the old one—we like this one better!' Rob had rolled his newspaper into a mock loudhailer and pretended to shout up to the sky.

Jen grabbed the loudhailer away from him and pretended to shout. 'Do you want a fresh cuppa? Hey, this will come in handy now that you're of, you know, advancing years.' Rob grabbed the newspaper and pretended to beat her with it, and Jen collapsed into fits of giggles. They stopped and smiled at each other, and both of their gazes fell back to the school report. Each picked up a sheet and began reading the comments again, sipping their tea in silence, Rob mouthing some of the words —reaffirming again that they said what they had ten minutes ago. Their son somehow, for some reason, had changed —and it was great.

Chapter 24

In Search of Proof

The electronic doors swished open and ushered Archie into the library. He moved quickly and purposefully, making a beeline for the familiar face of the librarian who had helped him with his research.

There was a small queue at the Enquiries Desk and she was helping people with their queries. Smiling, she looked up at Archie, recognised him, and gave him a wave. Archie reached up and waved enthusiastically, then checked himself as a few people turned and stared. Libraries weren't places for enthusiastic body language, he remembered, and actually—that wasn't his usual style. Not at all. He was too excited and nervous, too eager to get on with his quest to feel the old shyness and awkwardness which usually consumed him when surrounded by strangers, adults, and pretty much anyone other than his close mates.

It seemed like hours, but it was less than ten minutes which had passed, slowly, agonisingly, for Archie. At last, he stood in front of a smiling Mrs. Craigie. Her short, cropped, grey hair framed her bright, intelligent eyes and smiling face. She was small and used a step behind the counter to raise herself up to greet library customers. Archie had got quite a shock when she'd stepped down and walked around the tall counter to help him the first time. He stood taller than her, but she walked quickly, and he struggled to keep up as she began to navigate around tables and shelves. She turned to him, beckoning him to follow him, quickly.

'I know that you'll be after a computer, young man. Have you remembered your password?' She turned behind, smiling back at him.

'Yes, thanks.' Archie followed her trail, step-by-step, as she made her way up the long, silver, metal-framed staircase to the Information Suite.

'And you remember how to access our archives?' Archie had caught up with her and marched up the stairs by her side, making way for people walking down them on the other side of the staircase.

'Yes. I'm on to my last piece of research now.'

'Good. Well done! It makes my heart sing to see you so enthusiastic, especially after the tragic tale you uncovered. Well done for ploughing on, son. I wish more young people took such an interest.'

Archie muttered something in response, but his mind was now focused on the computer station where he'd been guided.

'You will remember to book next time, won't you?' Mrs. Craigie gave him a mock stern shake of the head, then smiled. 'I'll leave you to it, then; just shout up if you need help. I'll be stacking books on this floor—I'm just over there.'

Archie had already fallen into the task of logging in, and the librarian realised he was lost in his task. She smiled and shook her head, surprised, again, at his commitment and enthusiasm for his work. She wondered whether she should check with him about what school he attended. Perhaps she could write an e-mail or send a letter praising him for his work on his history project? She wandered away from Archie, who was staring intently at the screen. He was checking his login information and archive files' instructions, which he'd written in his notebook, along with his research.

Archie talked to himself as he flicked through pages of archives, desperately searching for the precious jewel of information. His stomach churned; his palms sweated. *Could this be real?* It was real... He knew and yet, changing events. Changing... history. In spite of all that had happened, it still seemed—surreal.

'North Shields Gazette... 1940s... 1941... October ... Got it.'

Archie's eyes scoured the pages. He scanned down the page, and it appeared. The story. The photograph. The same date. The same image of a house half in ruins. But this time, it was different.

Now, in front of the ruins stood the family: Maggie, Lou and Arthur. Arthur's hand was held in a thumb's up gesture, and Maggie and Lou smiled broadly at the camera. The headline, Archie realised, was different. 'Schoolboy hero saves family's lives!'

Archie felt his eyes swell with tears. He bent forward and rested his head in both hands and felt warm tears seep through the small gaps between his fingers. He pushed his chair back and laid his body back, staring at the bright, spot-lighted ceiling. Mrs. Craigie had been peering over, watching his intent search, and she now saw Archie, crying, almost overcome with emotion. She walked towards him, ready to comfort him, then stopped. Perhaps he needed a moment, she halted in her step and turned back to her work.

Archie stayed motionless, then felt laughter begin to bubble up from somewhere deep within him. He lay forward, respectful of his surroundings, and his shoulders heaved with short bursts of laughter— hysteria, he realised. Relief-induced hysteria.

He pulled his chair towards the computer, and read the story carefully, in full. It detailed Arthur's moonlight adventure with Lou, Maggie and June's pursuit—and the perfect timing of it. Maggie was interviewed, 'I was so mad at him. But look what he did! He's our hero; he saved us all!'

Archie stared at the picture. Arthur, fair, smiling, freckled, looked nothing like Archie. A glance could tell you of Arthur's friendliness, his good nature. Archie realised he would miss him, miss being him. He'd miss Maggie and Lou, and... their lives. But he smiled, widely... a broad, unshielded, Arthur Dennison grin. And as he did so, he shut down the computer, and slowly stood up.

Archie tucked his notebook and pen into his coat pocket and saw Mrs. Craigie looking over at him. She mouthed, 'Are you all right?' to him, across the library floor and Archie grinned, widely, and gave her a thumbs-up sign. She nodded and gave him a slightly puzzled smile, and a wave. Archie waved back and made his way across the library, to the stairs; he felt like he was floating. He found himself outside. He felt like he was walking on air. He'd heard that expression before but hadn't experienced it, not really. He'd been elated after scoring a winning goal or winning a computer game, but not like this. This was a nothing-in-the-whole-world-can-bother-me feeling.

And he liked it.

Chapter 25

Blue Skies

Twenty minutes later, Archie stood in the mid-day sun, shielded his eyes and stared up at the roof of his house. The same fault in the brickwork, the same join, the same damage. But he could look at it now without his stomach flipping in concern and worry; they had survived.

Archie used his key and whistled his way down the corridor. Music flooded out from the kitchen; the door was ajar. He took off his coat, dutifully hanging it up instead of throwing it over the bannister, as was his usual habit, and stopped. The music. He recognised it... But it couldn't be. He checked his surroundings: wooden flooring, his dad's boots under the coat hooks—full of modern-day jackets and his mam's scarves. He was home, his home, his modern-day home. But the music...

'Don't sit under the apple tree...'

The Andrews Sisters sang out and the tune rang down this passage way. He shook his head in wonderment and opened the kitchen door. Jen was preparing a salad, and Rob was sitting at the breakfast bar, reading the newspaper. They shared a glance, as Archie began to sing along with the tune—reaching for the kettle, matching the war-time melody word-for-word. The music finished and the D.J. cut in, but not until Archie had joined in the final chorus, grabbing his mother and dancing her around the kitchen. Jen was amazed, and Rob's head shook in surprise as he laid down his newspaper, once again.

'Right then, who wants a cup of tea?' Archie asked.

Rob and Jen stared at each other, and Archie fell to making the tea, still whistling the tune to himself.

Life was good, he realised. He was here; everyone was safe—everyone. And the future was... bright.

About The Author

Andrea Hewitson was born in Newcastle upon Tyne and has lived in the North East her whole life. She started her career working in the NHS in clerical jobs, but left to study a degree course in English and History in the late 1990s. Having worked as an English Teacher in secondary education, she is now semi-retired.

She has a passion for history and literature, and she has dabbled in writing for about ten years.

This novella was inspired by a visit with her husband to Hexham Abbey in 2013. On a tour of the Abbey, their guide showed them a glass case containing many paper aeroplanes which were intricately decorated in pencil: all World War Two fighter craft. These had been found under the floor of the choir stalls: it seems the choir boys were not paying close attention to all of the choral training!

And so, this story of time travel, local experiences during World War Two and Archie's 'journey' was born.

You can contact Andrea at toffee14565@gmail.com.
www.andreahewitson.com